AMULET BOOKS
NEW YORK

the
LAST
THING
you
said

SARA BIREN

Cataloging-in-Publication Data has been applied for
and may be obtained from the Library of Congress.

ISBN: 978-1-4197-2304-9

ABRAMS The Art of Books
115 West 18th Street, New York, NY 10011
abramsbooks.com

In Memory of Nicole

and for everyone who loved and misses her

What is life? It is the flash of a firefly in the night.
It is the breath of a buffalo in the wintertime.
It is the little shadow which runs across the
grass and loses itself in the sunset.

—*Crowfoot*

MAY

Friendship is a single soul dwelling in two bodies.
—*Aristotle*

1 · Lucy

THIS CAN ONLY GET EASIER.

It's my first day at the resort, at the summer job I didn't want but took because I couldn't find a way to say no.

Emily pokes my arm. "Lucy?"

"Hmm?" I look down at the little girl. We sit on the sidewalk in front of her house, a bucket of colored chalk next to her. She holds a bright blue piece in one hand and shields her eyes from the sun with the other as she looks up at me.

"Can I have a drink?"

I tug on one of her blond pigtails. "Your water bottle is on the porch," I say, and she hops up.

Emily turned five a few weeks ago. She's a smart girl and knew a hundred words by the time she was two—I know because Trixie and I made a list. Emily is Trixie's cousin. We used to babysit her together; now it's only Emily and me.

It's the Saturday of Mother's Day weekend, fishing opener. A teaser—soon summer will arrive here in Halcyon Lake and hundreds of other small Minnesota resort towns like ours in the land of 11,842 lakes. School will end, and our sleepy little town will wake up, overrun with tourists.

Trixie's aunt and uncle—Emily's parents—own the Cabins at Apple Tree Lane. It's been in their family for generations, just like my family's restaurant. My job here is to take care of Emily and help out with housekeeping and light maintenance

1

at the resort. I'll pick up as many shifts as I can at the restaurant, too, to help out.

Busy is good.

"Lucy?" Emily has gotten her water bottle and set it on the sidewalk next to her colorful chalk drawings of misshapen butterflies. "Can we go swimming today?"

It's spring, too early for swimming. And even though I grew up splashing around the lake in my backyard, fishing and water-skiing and tubing, I've never been much of a swimmer. Even before.

Trixie was a champion swimmer, strong and fast, a fish streaking through the water.

"Ooh, too cold," I say.

"Lucy?"

"Yes, Emily?"

"Tell me a *Trixie*."

I smile. This has become one of our favorite activities, a way I can keep Trixie alive. The stories I tell Emily about her cousin have become a part of our routine.

"Once upon a time—" I start.

"There lived a happy little girl named Beatrix."

"But everyone called her Trixie."

"And she had a brother named Ben."

"Right," I say. "She had a brother named Ben." My throat tightens a little at his name.

"Tell me the first one, the first *Trixie*." Emily laughs, a dramatic ha-ha-ha with her hands on her stomach. She's playing along. This is how the *Trixies* go. I only tell the happy *Trixies*.

"One day, when Trixie was five years old, she went to kindergarten—"

"And she met Lulu. Lulu! That's you."

I smile. That first day of school, I was so nervous, I threw up on Trixie's shoes, but she wanted to be my friend anyway.

I wasn't Lulu yet, not when we met. It was Trixie who first called me Lulu—then Ben and their parents. I felt special, unique, remarkable. So much more than boring Lucy. Even as we got older, when I was with the Porters, I was Lulu.

It was like I was a part of their family.

No one calls me Lulu now.

A car pulls into the driveway, a 1989 Formula 350 Firebird, black.

"Ben!" Emily squeals, and hops up again. "Ben's here."

Ben. Ben's here. My heart sinks to my toes and rebounds back up to my throat.

I swallow, stand up, and brush my chalky hands together.

I can almost hear Trixie's voice in my head: *Be really brave, Lulu.*

Her voice, vibrant and silvery, is fading.

Emily stands on the sidewalk to wait for Ben. She hops up and down, first on both feet, then alternating. She squeals again as he comes around the front of the car, tapping his knuckles twice against the gleaming hood, and crosses the driveway to her. I move closer to the porch, hoping to disappear into the whitewashed, morning-glory-covered lattice.

I love to spend time with this sweet, funny little girl who is now the age I was when I met her cousin, my very best friend in the world. There is always a nagging feeling that Ben will show up when I'm with her, though. The fear. The small hope.

"Ben!" Emily screams as he scoops her up in a hug. He is tall, with broad shoulders and lean, muscular arms. A swimmer, like his sister. When he lifts Emily above his head, his blue St. Croix Rod T-shirt hikes up, and I catch a glimpse of his smooth stomach above the waistline of his ratty cargo shorts. He's already tan, his hair washed out to a light brown, curls sticking out the sides of his baseball cap.

"Hi, Miss Emily."

Be really brave.

BRB—our code.

It's what Trixie used to say when I needed an extra push—to climb the stairs of the tall slide in the school playground, to leap onto a balance beam, to climb the one hundred thirty steps to the top of the Fire Tower.

It was all worth it—the rush, the gymnastics medals and accolades, the view from the Fire Tower, my world stretched out before me, Halcyon Lake and miles of jack pines and all the places I loved.

Those things were easy compared to this.

You should tell Ben how you feel. It will be worth it.

He notices me, glances in my direction and away in half a second. My heart skips, and I let myself think he might smile at me like he used to, his deep brown eyes flashing.

"Oh, hey, Lucy," he says, his voice dull and flat. "What are you doing here?"

Lucy. Not Lulu. Not anymore.

"Lucy's my babysitter," Emily says.

He drops her back down to the sidewalk. "Oh, yeah. I always forget."

"No you don't!" Emily cries. "Are you going fishing?"

"Yep. Where's your dad?"

"Dunno." Emily plops down and picks up her chalk to finish coloring in the bright blue wings of a butterfly.

"I gotta go. See you later, Emily." Ben's so good with her. She adores him.

I haven't said one word. The pounding of my heart in my ears slows and melts a little. My wonderful Ben.

No, that's not right. Ben is not mine. He is not wonderful, not anymore.

He walks around the other side of the garage to the path that leads to the resort and the lake. He doesn't look at me again. He doesn't say good-bye.

It wasn't always like this, back when we were friends, back when I thought someday we might be more than friends. Before Trixie died. I miss him, I miss him as much as I miss Trixie. Sometimes I catch him looking at me, and I wonder if he misses me, too.

I slip my hand into the pocket of my jeans. It's there—Ben's agate, smooth, cool to the touch. I flip the agate again and again between my thumb and index finger.

I wish I could find a way to get Ben Porter out of my heart.

2 · Ben

It's 9:54 and I'm late for work. Well, technically not late, except that my uncle believes that if you're not ten minutes early, you're late. So my ten A.M. shift really began at 9:50. Mum and Dad give me a hard time about driving here—I mean, it's a five-minute walk, max—but it's hard enough for me to get here on time as it is. John will shake his head, but what's he going to do, fire me?

Some days I wish he would. I wish I would get kicked out of school, I wish I could get the hell out of this town.

But Lulu—no, Lucy—is here.

I mean, she's *here*, sitting on my uncle's front sidewalk.

Lucy's the last thing I need today. I want to spend the day out on the lake, not worry about anything, not think about anything, and there she is with my cousin. Emily laughs at something Lucy says, and Lucy has this sort of half smile on her face.

It's been a long time since I've seen Lucy smile. Maybe she smiles, but not around me. God, I used to love her smile. The way it sort of creeps up on one side first, tentative, and then goes full out, lighting up her whole face.

I walk down the hill as fast as I can, away from Lucy and Emily. Trixie should be here watching Em, not Lucy. I'm a prick for thinking it. And it's not the first time.

We're not friends and it's my fault. You can't be a complete ass to someone and expect her to act like you weren't.

What does she think about when she sees me? Does she remember all the fun we had together—all those times fishing off the dock, all the talks we had on the Lazy River at the water park—or has she pushed it out of her mind? Does she think only about my sister? Does she hate me for what I did? For what I couldn't do?

For what I said?

I don't like to think about it. Our school schedules are different enough, and I usually don't see her much. But today, with Lucy here, everything about that day forces its way back. I think about how Trixie slipped away from us. And I think about what happened *after* that day, too, the day of her funeral, and how I screwed up everything.

Lucy must hate the sight of me, and I don't blame her. Most days, I hate the sight of me, too.

John waits for me on the dock with a guy in a goofy straw hat and a couple of kids, maybe around ten and twelve years old.

"You're late," John says under his breath. "It's 10:01."

"Sorry about that, folks," I say, and I step into the boat.

The weather is good—partly sunny, streaks of white clouds, a cool spring breeze. We head out to one of John's secret sweet spots. It's too early for bluegills, but we might be able to bring in a few crappies. There's a chill out here on the lake, so I pull on my ratty army-green Rapala hoodie. An image comes to me, and I suck in a breath: Lucy wearing it, standing on the rocky shore of Lake Superior, orange streaks of sunrise glistening on the water behind her.

I close my eyes against the memory. I've got to get her out of my head.

The dad knows a thing or two about fishing, but the boys whine and give him a ton of attitude. I help them bait and untangle their lines for what seems like hours but is probably only about forty-five minutes. They throw night crawlers at each other. They both catch a couple of crappies and then fight over which one is bigger.

Trixie and I fought like that, too, when we were their age.

"Dad," the older one whines, "this is so boring. Let's go."

"Yeah," says the younger one, "and it stinks out here."

After a few more minutes of the kids pissing and moaning, the dad gives in and John pulls up anchor.

The ride back to shore won't take long, but John slows the boat to a crawl when he sees a family of loons. We watch as they drift across the lake, dive down, resurface.

Moments like this, when I'm out on the lake, I can pretend that nothing has changed, that life is all sunshine and roses and shit like that. It doesn't last. I can't live my life out on a boat in the middle of Halcyon Lake.

I miss my sister. We fought a lot and gave each other grief. Most days she irritated the hell out of me, but every day without her sucks.

3 · Lucy

AFTER LUNCH, EMILY AND I CLIMB UP TO THE TREE HOUSE. Seven rickety two-by-fours nailed to the trunk of a box elder tree in the backyard lead to a platform with mismatched plywood walls and an upside-down *V* for a roof. Her dad, John, and his brother, Tom—Trixie's dad—built the tree house when they were kids and there haven't been many improvements to it since.

My foot slips on the loose step halfway up, but I take a deep breath and continue the climb. This is nothing. I've done this a thousand times. If I can climb the Fire Tower, I can do this. I tighten my grip on the wood.

Emily's already dealt out a game of Go Fish by the time I pull myself up onto the platform. I sit across from her. From here, I can see down the hill to the resort, can see Ben as he walks up from the lake. My heart does its usual nosedive. Crash and burn.

Ben was the first boy I ever loved. The only boy I've ever loved. My first kiss.

I always thought that Trixie would be around for that, Trixie who had watched me fall more in love with her brother every day. But she wasn't.

There are *Trixies* I don't tell Emily, like the one about the day she died.

The four of us—me, Trixie, Ben, and my brother, Clayton—are lying on the float. The sun is strong. I'm sleepy and hazy and in love with the boy lying next to me, so close our hands almost touch.

"It's hot," Trixie says. I feel her sit up next to me. "Let's swim out to the island."

"No," Ben says. "I'm sleeping. Go away."

"You're not sleeping," Trixie says. "I know you're not. Now Clayton—he's sleeping. Listen to that snore."

I don't open my eyes. The insides of my eyelids are red, red, red from the sun. I wish Ben and I were here alone. I would stay all day.

Trixie doesn't ask me to swim to the island. She knows how much I hate the weeds that snake out of nowhere to tangle around your ankles. It was hard enough for me to swim out to the raft.

"Should we go home?" she asks.

Now I sit up. I angle to face her and pull my knees up, put my arms around them.

"No," I whisper. "I'm not ready to go home."

She winks at me, then nudges Clay's ankle with her foot. "Clayton? Race you to the island?"

My brother pops up. "What? What did I miss? You want to race me, ya little punk?" He reties the drawstring on his trunks and jumps into the water, a cannonball, splashing water across the swim float. The cool spray feels refreshing on my hot skin.

"It's a good day to have a good day." She leans in close to me and whispers, "BRB, Lucy. Promise me."

"The best day," I say. "I promise."

Trixie dives into the lake. Ben and I are quiet. I can hear both our breaths, our heartbeats, even over the noise of the lake, the splashing, the laughter.

Ben sits up.

He reaches out and tugs at my ponytail.

Then he runs his hand down the side of my arm. I gasp; shivers overtake me in the hot, hot sun.

"Lulu," he says. "Look at me."

But I don't. I can't.

I hold my breath as Ben strokes his index finger against my arm again. "Lulu, I've been wondering if—"

He is cut off by the sound of Clayton shouting from the lake.

Ben dives into the water and swims toward the island, toward Clay, toward where Trixie should be. Ben resurfaces, shouts, *I can't see her, call for help.* I splash to shore, crying, shaking. A woman puts a towel around my shoulders, says she's already called 911, tells me to breathe.

Breathe.

I don't tell Emily this story, but someday I will. Someday she will want to know all the sad parts, too, not just the happy, silly stories of two girls growing up.

When Tami gets home from running errands, Ben's car is no longer in the driveway. She asks if I'd like a ride home since it's been drizzling off and on the last couple of hours, but I tell her I'll swing by the Full Loon and catch a ride with my mom.

"You'll be lucky if they don't toss you an apron and put you to work," Tami says. "It's opener weekend. And your mom told me that Rita quit."

I roll my eyes. "Not much of a loss, if you ask me." Mom had called me in countless times to cover for Rita at the last minute, but she completely freaked out when her most veteran waitress left them high and dry.

The Full Loon Café, the restaurant that's been in my mom's family since the 1940s, isn't far from the resort. Nothing's far from anything in this town. The café parking lot is crowded; even the overflow lot behind the Oasis gas station is packed with vehicles. A half-dozen people crowd onto the two wooden benches next to the front door, waiting for a table. Saturday night, fishing opener, Mom's down a full-timer, and her summer part-timers are new and green.

I should go in, grab an apron, and help them out of the weeds.

But I don't.

I keep walking, past the café and the Oasis, through our touristy downtown with its candy store and T-shirt shop and old-fashioned, single-screen movie theater.

I speed up as I walk past Ben's house. The house where he grew up with Trixie. The house where I spent so much time— sleepovers and birthdays and special days and ordinary days— like I was part of their family.

There have been days since when I walk past that house and wish, wish, wish that I were brave enough to stop, to touch the wheels of Trixie's bike, still hanging on its hooks in the garage, to have tea with Jane, Trixie's mom. To ask her for the Book of Quotes, the notebook Trixie and I filled with lyrics and quotations and poems.

Brave enough to talk to Ben, more than the tense, polite things we say to each other when it can't be avoided. More than the shallow "How've you been," when really I want to reach into his heart and ask him everything.

He told me once that I could ask him anything, one night last summer before Trixie died—a game we played to keep me from freaking out as we climbed the one hundred thirty steps of the Fire Tower.

"What's your middle name?" I asked.

"Alistair. Didn't you already know that?" He stood close behind me on the steps, like he'd block me from falling backward.

I did know. His full name, Bennett Alistair Porter. His birthday, April 11.

"Were you named for anyone?"

"Yes. My grandfather's name is Alistair."

"Favorite meal?"

"Mum's fish-and-chips."

"Favorite candy?"

"Maple fudge." I could hear the smile in his words.

At this, I stumbled a little, and he put his hands on my waist to steady me. I was glad that he was behind me, that he couldn't see my face, hot with embarrassment and from his touch.

Now, down the block from the Porters' house, I sigh with relief that no one was home. I wouldn't have been brave enough to stop anyway.

The First Day of Kindergarten

Once upon a time, there lived a happy little girl named Beatrix, but everyone called her Trixie. Trixie lived with her mum and her dad and her big brother, Ben.

One day, when Trixie was five years old, she went to kindergarten. She knew all the other children in her class, from church and the park and preschool, except for one little girl with curly brown pigtails. And on that first day of school, Trixie marched right over to the girl with the pigtails and stuck out her hand.

"Hello, I'm Trixie. What's your name?" she asked.

"My name is Lucy," the little girl said. She was very nervous, even though Trixie smiled at her.

And that's when the little girl named Lucy threw up all over Trixie's shoes.

Trixie was very nice to Lucy. She called for the teacher and rubbed Lucy's back and said, "You're fine. You're fine."

"Trixie," said their teacher, "please take Lucy to the nurse."

The nurse called Lucy's mother, and Trixie waited with her in the office until her mother arrived.

"I'm going to call you Lulu," Trixie said as they sat side by side in yellow plastic chairs.

"Why?" Lucy asked.

"Because you look like a Lulu."

The next day, Lucy, now called Lulu, wasn't nervous about kindergarten. Trixie and Lulu built a village with blocks and played kitchen and practiced writing their names. They swung together on the monkey bars. They sat next to each other during snack time. Everywhere that Trixie and Lulu went, everything they touched was left with a fine dusting of silver and gold glitter.

"Bye, Lulu," Trixie said at the end of the day. "I can't wait for us to be friends again tomorrow and the next day and forever."

She squeezed Lulu's hand, and when she let go, Lulu traced the line of glimmering gold across her palm that sealed their friendship forever.

4 · Ben

At dinner, Dad talks nonstop.

"The lake was pretty crowded today, don't you think, Ben? Beautiful day. The resort's booked up for the summer already, and most of them want guides, too. Lots of fishing in our future."

Fishing is one of the few things we have in common anymore, although it's not like it used to be. Nothing is. Dad and Uncle John grew up at the resort and know every single inch of Halcyon Lake like the backs of their hands—the widemouth sweet spots and the best weed beds for bluegills. Dad works at the resort during the summer, too, when he's off from his job teaching earth science at the middle school.

Mum sets a platter of brownies on the table. Today her blond hair is a perfect wave held back with a headband that matches her light blue blouse. Mum is from London, and she's got the accent and obsessions with Jane Austen and gardens to go along with it.

"I spent the morning working up at the cemetery," Mum says when Dad finally stops rambling. Like she's gone to the grocery store or the library. A common errand. "A few of the bricks around Mr. Wilson's garden had come loose, so I fixed those and weeded a bit."

Not only has my mother planted a garden for Trixie, she tends to neglected graves, too. She's gone to the cemetery almost every day since Trixie died, even in winter.

"You should come with me, Ben," Mum says. "It would be good for you to help with your sister's garden. I find that digging in the earth to make room for something beautiful is rather therapeutic."

Sure. Sometimes she comes back, her face streaked with dirt and tears, and she drinks cup after cup of tea. Incapable of doing anything else, her energy and emotions used up in the dirt.

"I'll stick to fishing," I say, "but thanks."

"I'm with you there, son," Dad says.

"Is that right?" I mumble. I can't remember the last time my dad and I fished together.

Mum sighs. Dad clears his throat and takes a drink from a bottle of beer. He never used to drink at dinner. Now he keeps the fridge and liquor cabinet stocked. It's convenient for me when he forgets to lock it.

"I saw Lucy Meadows up at the resort today," Dad says. "She's helping out with Emily this summer."

I can barely swallow the last of my hamburger, suddenly dry and tasteless. I take a long drink of water. I don't say anything.

I guess I do remember the last time I went out fishing with my dad.

Of course it was last summer, before Trixie died. Our family and the Meadows family had gone out on the pontoon. Trixie fell asleep in the sun but Lucy fished. She sat next to me on one of the chairs in the bow, propped her feet on the edge of the boat, and waited. She always had more patience than Trix. She reeled in some perch and a nice smallmouth bass.

"That poor girl," Mum says.

That's something I don't get about my mother—how she is always so concerned about Lucy, how Lucy's doing. If it were me, I'd be pissed. I'd be thinking all the time: *Lucy is alive but my daughter isn't.*

Lucy is alive but my sister isn't. Maybe if I'd paid more attention that day, instead of thinking about Lucy—that she was so close, that her skin was so warm, glistening in the sun— maybe Trixie would be alive.

Guilt bubbles its way up my throat like acid.

"How's Clayton doing at university, Ben?" Mum asks. Her words jar me from my memories.

"I don't know," I say and stand up. "How would I know? I have to go."

"What do you mean, how would you know? You *should* know. Clayton is one of your best friends," Mum says.

"Not anymore," I mumble.

He started school a couple of weeks after Trixie died. He got out of town and doesn't come back much. It's easier this way, for him and for me.

"Well, what about Lucy? I wish you'd invite her over for dinner sometime. I'd love to see her."

"Mum," I say, the word heavy, like a stone. Like I'd ever invite Lucy over for dinner. God, what do I have to do to get her to stop already? "I really have to go."

"Ben," she says, "what about Lucy? Will you ask her to dinner?"

Fuck no, I won't ask her to dinner.

Mum's jaw drops and Dad stands up and I realize then that I said it out loud.

"Ben, apologize to your mother," Dad says.

Now I'm pissed. I'm pissed at myself and at Mum for keeping at me, and I'm pissed at Dad, too, for bringing up Lucy in the first place.

"Fuck it." I push back my chair and walk out.

"Ben," Mum calls, and there's pain in her voice.

"Come back here and—" Dad's words are cut off by the slam of the door as I go out to the garage.

5 · *Lucy*

HANNAH CALLS ME AS I WALK ONTO THREE CROWS LANE FROM the main road, almost home.

"Hey, whatcha doing?" she asks. She moved here before school started this year from Mitchell, South Dakota, home of the World's Only Corn Palace, and has a mellow SoDak twang.

The walk from town has been warm, the air thick with rain and humidity. I'm out of breath.

"Just getting home," I say.

"Did you see Ben today?" She smacks her lips. "Mwah, mwah!"

We've become friends during the school year, and I've tried and tried to explain about Ben without explaining too much. But she won't give up. I don't answer.

"So that's a yes, then. Was he wearing that gray ringer T-shirt? He looks so totally hot in that. Well, in anything, really, although I'd rather see him *without* a shirt."

"God, Hannah," I say. "Stop already."

"Whatever. We both know you're totally in love with him, Lucille. Give in to your feelings."

If only it were that easy.

If only she would stop saying things like that.

"Whatever," she says again. "You were supposed to call me when you were done babysitting. Remember? Movie night."

"Oh. Sorry, long day. Too many distractions."

"I'll bet. What time should I pick you up? The movie starts in, like, forty-five minutes. Are you ready or what?"

"I'm almost home. Give me fifteen minutes to shower, and I'll meet you out front."

I'm surprised to see Dad's truck in the driveway. He's been pulling a lot of weekend shifts at the plant. The driveway splits off to the right to our neighbors' house, the Clarks', and next to their old brown Buick is a car I've never seen before. A silver Volvo—sleek, urban, out of place.

"Dad?" I call as I open the front door, but there's no answer. I run up the stairs and pull a fresh T-shirt and skirt from a laundry basket on the floor and take a quick shower, not bothering to wash my hair. There isn't time to blow-dry it so it won't frizz. I twist it into a messy bun and secure it with a clip.

As I sort through a porcelain dish of earrings to find a matching pair, I nearly tip over the framed photo next to it—a picture Ben took of Trixie and me at Canal Park in Duluth last summer, laughing and squinting into the sun, the Aerial Lift Bridge behind us.

I touch my fingers to the photo.

Both of those girls are gone.

Tucked into the corner of the frame is the memorial card from her funeral. I pick it up and open it to the George Bernard Shaw quote inside: *Life is no "brief candle" for me. It is a sort of splendid torch which I have got hold of for the moment, and I want to make it burn as brightly as possible.*

It was the first quote Trixie wrote in our Book of Quotes, followed by song lyrics and movie quotes and funny things we said—her handwriting large and loopy, mine small, careful.

I walk downstairs and step out onto the deck, looking for my dad. He's in the backyard, down the hill at our lakeside patio with the Clarks and two people I don't know—a tall woman in a flowing peasant skirt and a boy who's even taller.

Dad sees me, waves, and starts up the hill, motioning for me to come down. I meet him halfway.

"Where've you been? Come meet the Stanfords."

"Who are the Stanfords?"

"The renters."

"The renters?"

"Yeah, Betty and Ron are spending the summer in Canada at their daughter's, remember? And they're renting out their house."

"Oh, right." I remember Betty mentioning something about that the last time she brought over a plate of cookies. Ron and Betty are like an extra set of grandparents. Betty loves her baked goods and we benefit from it.

"Her son's about your age, I think," Dad says as we walk toward the patio.

I squint as we get closer. The boy—the *cute* boy—stands at the fire pit. His shaggy blond hair sticks out in several directions. He's wearing baggy black cargo shorts and a Dr Pepper T-shirt torn at the hem. He pulls a hand out of his pocket and raises it in a wave.

Betty pulls me into a hug. Her gray-haired head comes up

to about my shoulders and she always smells like cinnamon rolls. "Hello, Luce," she says, her Canadian *ooo* long and bottomless. "These are the Stanfords. They're staying at our place this summer."

The woman in the peasant skirt reaches out her hand. Her skin is soft, and her long fingers are covered with silver and black rings. She smells earthy.

"Lucy, such a pleasure. I'm Shay and this is my son, Simon."

Dr Pepper—Simon—grins and raises his eyebrows.

"Hey," he says.

"Mrs. Stanford is an artist," Ron says.

"That's *Ms.* Stanford," the woman says, "but please call me Shay."

"So," my dad says in a big voice, "Shay asked if it would be okay if she could work down here at the patio since there's only the dock next door. That's okay with you, right, Luce? Let's take a quick tour of the yard and the lakeshore before you folks get on the road."

Excuse me? She wants to use our patio as an art studio? Our patio, with its starburst pavers and fire pit and comfy Adirondack chairs, is where I go to escape, where I can think about Trixie and cry without anyone bothering me.

I shake my head. "Wish I could join you," I say in a false, cheerful voice. "Hannah's picking me up in a few minutes."

"Well, such a pleasure to meet you." Shay puts her hand on my arm. "I'm so looking forward to getting to know you better this summer."

The Clarks, my dad, and Shay turn to go down to the beach, but Simon stays behind.

He's definitely cute.

He's staring at me.

I'm having trouble looking away, my eyes locked on his intense green ones. Why is he staring at me?

Dr Pepper smiles. "Your place is really nice."

"Thanks . . . well, um, I should go," I say, but I don't move. I stand there and look up at him, and when he grins at me, I can't help it. I smile back.

"Have fun," he says.

"Did you know there's no period in Dr?" I ask, still not moving.

"What?" His eyes narrow in confusion.

I point at his shirt. "Dr Pepper. No period in *Dr*. We learned about it in history. The period was dropped in the 1950s, but I can't remember why."

He doesn't say anything, and I can feel my cheeks flame. Why do I have to be such a dork? *No period in Dr Pepper.* Honestly.

He's still smiling, though, and then he says, "You know, I wasn't really sure how I felt about leaving my friends for the summer and living up here in the middle of nowhere. Now that I've met you, things are definitely looking up."

"Uhh." Good one.

"I like you," he says. "You're spunky."

No one's ever called me spunky before.

"I really have to go. My friend'll be here soon and—"

"I'll keep you company while you wait," he says.

I bite back a smile.

We walk around the front of the house and sit on the porch steps. I pull out my cell phone. Hannah should be here by now. I'll give her five minutes before I call her to make sure she's okay.

Simon's sitting close, close enough that I can feel the heat from his pale arms, covered with fine blond hairs. His fingers are long, some smudged blue and black.

Why am I inspecting his fingers?

I look up. The smile hasn't left his face. He smells good, like oil paints and something spicy, a hint of cologne.

"What are you up to tonight?" His voice is warm and friendly.

"Movie."

"There's a theater in town?"

"Yeah," I say. "We may be a small town, but we *do* have a movie theater."

"Thank God," he says. "How many screens?"

"One."

He laughs, and I like the sound of it. "Seriously?"

"The theater was built in 1919. It's kind of a big deal."

"Cool. What's playing?"

I shrug. I have no idea. It doesn't matter, really. It's what we do on Saturday nights. "There are a couple of theaters down in Brainerd, too, if you need more variety."

"I don't know," he says slowly. "I have a feeling I won't be too bored this summer."

I hear the crunch of gravel as Hannah pulls into the driveway. I stand up. "She's here."

He stands up, too, and whistles as Hannah parks her mom's old Lexus in front of the garage. "Nice wheels."

"Well, thanks for keeping me company." I wave at him as I get into the car. He waves back.

Hannah grins at me. "Who's the hottie?"

My cheeks go red. "Betty and Ron are renting out their house this summer."

"To that guy?"

"Yeah, and his mom."

"Does he have a name?"

"Simon."

"Simon," she says, like she's trying it out. "Simon the Renter."

"Simon the Renter." I try it out, too.

"He's cute."

I shrug. "He's nice."

"Oh, girl, you are going to have fun this summer!"

Everything's fun for Hannah. Trixie was the same way.

I'm more realistic.

"Yes," I say, "I'm sure I'll have lots of time to hang out with Simon the Renter when I'm not working my two jobs."

"You never know."

Maybe. Simon's cute and friendly, but the best thing is that he's not from here.

He doesn't know about poor Lucy, the girl who lost her best friend.

"Guess what? My mom's going on a book tour this summer, and I get to come along, and guess where we're going? Texas!" She squeals. "Oh my God, what if I meet Tony Romo?"

I roll my eyes. Hannah's mom, Madeleine Mills, has written twenty-six bestselling historical western romances. Twenty-six. Each one sells more than the last, probably thanks in part to covers with bare-chested cowboys and women with bosoms bursting out of their pioneer frocks.

Hannah's bosom is pretty much bursting out of her own shirt tonight. She's wearing a pink cowboy hat, the brim low over her forehead, a fitted cream-colored eyelet tank, tight denim miniskirt, and her favorite boots, brown suede with fringe. She loves those boots enough that she would wear them to gym class if she could.

"Did I miss the memo to dress like a rodeo-ho?" I ask.

Hannah laughs as she rolls through a stop sign onto Main Street. Her dad competed on the professional rodeo circuit for a few years, and Hannah knows more about the sport than anyone I've ever met. As unlikely as it seems, Minnesota is home to dozens of rodeos every year, and she's been trying to get me to go to one since the day we met.

"Must have. But I believe the term you're looking for is buckle bunny, sweetheart. What do you call your ensemble? Laundry-basket chic?"

I laugh. "Exactly. How did you know?"

"Oh, I know you, Lucille. That skirt is too long. God, girl, show a little leg or something. What good is that hot gymnast bod if you don't show it off?"

My gymnast bod isn't as hot as it used to be. I quit the team after Trixie died. Not that there would have been the money for it anyway, not with Clay calling home and asking for money all the time on top of everything else.

Hannah pulls the Lexus into the parking lot across the street from the theater and leans forward to scan for a good spot.

"By the way," she says, "remember Dustin, that guy from Carly's party? He's meeting us here."

"Great." I pull the mirror down and tuck a loose curl behind my ear. "You two have fun."

"Oh, now, Lucille, don't be a party pooper!" She opens her door and gets out of the car.

It's been a long day. I'm tired, and I'm 99.9 percent sure that when I cross the street with Hannah to hang out with the crowd that's gathered under the marquee of the theater, Ben will be there. It's easy enough to try to pretend that he's not around at school. He's a junior; I'm a sophomore. We have different schedules. But on the weekends, it's hard not to run into him.

But it's not just Ben.

Ben will be there with Dana, his girlfriend.

Typical Saturday night in Halcyon Lake.

6 · Ben

I GET IN THE FIREBIRD AND DRIVE.

I'm in the parking lot at the Fire Tower before I even know where I'm going.

The lot is empty—not that there are ever a lot of cars here this time of night. Later, after the movie's over, and in the fall after football games, that's when the lot fills up.

Right now, I've got the place to myself.

I reach into the backseat for my hiking boots and once I've got them on, I hit the trail. It's a good hike up a steep hill to get to the tower, and by the time I reach it, I'm breathing heavily.

Shit, I need to start training again.

The tower looms tall against the trees and inky blue sky. I start to climb, gripping the handrails as the tower sways in the wind. This thing isn't called "historic" for nothing.

It's a long way up.

I reach the top and stand near the railing, looking out over the roads and trees and lakes, and I realize that I've never been up here alone.

It's quiet and peaceful high above the treetops, but I don't feel that way inside. I don't remember what it's like to live without the clutch of guilt and sorrow around my neck.

At Trixie's funeral, I greeted the hundreds of people who came to the church to offer their kind words and clichés. I nodded my head, said, "Thank you for coming," and "That's so kind of you," a million times.

Then it was over, and Lucy and I were the last ones in the church basement.

And I remember thinking, *Lulu is the only good thing about today. She is the only good thing about my life.*

We walked out to the parking lot so I could drive her home. She didn't want to get in the front seat of the Firebird and I understood that. Sitting there, without Trixie to ride shotgun, meant that it was real. The funeral, the casket in front of us, the sound of the dirt hitting the top of it—all of that was real, expected.

This was not expected. We had not factored this into the plan.

This was how our lives would be now, the subtle differences along with the obvious ones.

"It's okay," I told her, and she slid in, crying.

She'd cried so much. I wished I knew a way to help her.

We sat in her driveway for a long time, not talking, the rain landing in sheets across my windshield, the wipers on double time until I flicked them off, pointless because we weren't moving, and she started to cry again and I couldn't bear it.

So I reached out my hand and gently turned her head so that she faced me, and I wiped away tears with the pad of my thumb. I leaned in and did what I'd wanted to do for weeks.

I kissed her.

I kissed Lulu and it was a perfect moment, perfect, until I fucked it up.

She pulled away from me, stunned, her eyes wide.

"Why did you do that?" she asked me, her voice brittle. She sounded so young at that moment. So hurt.

"Lulu," I said, "you know why." I couldn't say it, but she had to know. It had been there between us all summer. I had started to tell her on the swim float. I put my hand on hers, but she pulled it away.

"We shouldn't, Ben. Not today." Her voice was barely above a whisper.

Bile rose in my throat, and I was overcome with dread and guilt and anger.

Filled with a terrible, inexplicable need to hurt her.

I slammed my hands against the steering wheel.

"You're right," I said, my voice cold. "This was a mistake. We shouldn't be here. Trixie shouldn't be dead. But she is. I couldn't save her. And we both know why."

"What?" she whispered. "What do you mean?"

"I couldn't save her. I didn't get to her in time. If you hadn't been there, I would have."

She didn't say a word. She looked at me with those wide eyes that filled with tears once again until the pools overflowed onto her cheeks.

And I kept going. "All of this is your fault."

"Why are you saying this?" she cried.

"It's true. And you know it."

"Ben—" she began, but a sob shook her body and she dropped her head in her hands.

"I hate this," I said. "I hate that you're here and she isn't. Get the fuck out of my car."

And she did. She opened the door and stumbled across the driveway in the heavy rain, her feet bare, her plain black pumps gripped tightly against her chest.

The pain of losing Trixie was too much—I had to give some of it away. So I gave it to Lucy, who more than anyone didn't deserve such a terrible thing. I should have told her that if I could, I would take away *her* pain. Because my own was so unbearable, what difference would it have made if I could have cut hers in half and taken it for myself?

Instead, I gave her more.

For one moment, she turned to look back at me before she opened the door, a moment that I could have gone to her through the rain and the mud and told her I didn't mean it, told her that I was crazy with grief and sadness, begged for her forgiveness.

But I didn't.

And I've lived with it every moment since then.

My cell phone buzzes three times, fast. I pull it out of my pocket and check my messages.

One from Guthrie. *Dude u got trouble. Dana pist.*

Two from Dana.

Where r u? I'm @ the theater.

Ben, you promised.

Shit. Shitshitshit.

I take one last look across the treetops and try again to find some peace in the silence and solitude. There is nothing, and

I can't escape the reality that waits for me at the bottom of the tower. I turn and begin the climb back down.

When I get to the theater, everyone is inside except for Dana. She's alone, leaning against the wall, her arms crossed. Guthrie was right. She is *pist*.

Here's how it goes down:

Dana: You're late. You promised me you wouldn't be late, Ben.

Me (swats at a swarm of gnats): Sorry. Got tied up at the resort.

Dana: Oh.

Me: You don't believe me?

Dana: Of course I do!

Me: Doesn't seem like it.

Dana: Ben, I'm trying to *help*. You seem so, I don't know, lost lately *(puts hand on my arm)*.

Me: Dana—

Dana (in a soft, low voice): I wish you would let me help you.

Me (pulls arm away): What makes you think I need help?

Dana (pinches lips together): You have no idea how many people *care* about you, Benjamin. How many people *love* you. How many people *ache* for you because you're in *so* much pain—

Me (interrupts, angry, sick of the drama, sick of hearing her talk in italics all the time): Shut up.

Dana (mouth drops open): What? What did you say?

Me (takes a step back): I said shut up. You want to help me? You can help me by shutting the hell up.

Dana (takes a step toward me, panicked): You don't mean that. You *can't possibly* mean that.

Me (raises one eyebrow, takes another step backward): Oh, I mean it. And my name is not fucking Benjamin.

I'm a dick and she's too nice. She shouldn't put up with my shit.

I walk across the parking lot and get in the Firebird. It takes about five seconds for Dana to decide to follow me.

"Let's drive around," she says. "Maybe it will clear your head."

I know where this is going.

"Fine."

We drive to the abandoned baseball fields behind the paper mill. I park the car and turn toward the girl in the front seat. My girlfriend. She smiles. Her teeth are artificially perfect and white. In fact, she has no visible flaws. Her hair, her smile, her GPA, everything is perfect. A little too perfect, maybe.

Lucy's ponytails are usually crooked or she'll miss a few strands that curl around her neck or one side will be bumpy. And if you look closely, you can see that one of Lucy's blue eyes is narrower at the outside corner than the other. Two of her bottom teeth are crooked, angled slightly, bowing to each other.

I'm sitting in my car with my girlfriend, thinking about Lucy Meadows.

I don't want to think anymore.

So I don't. I lean over to Dana.

That's how it works with us. I do something to piss Dana off, we fight about it, we bail on our friends, we drive around, we fool around in my car.

And I feel nothing. Empty. The way I like it.

Dana wasn't the first one. First there was Anna. Anna did that thing—put her hand on my arm, tilted her head, used that low voice—right after Trixie died. She cornered me during study hall on the first day of school. She said she was so sorry about Trixie and Trixie was a wonderful friend and we were all going to miss Trixie so very much.

She said my sister's name so many times I wanted to twist her head right off her neck.

Anna wasn't friends with Trix.

Then her voice got even lower and she said, "I'm worried about you. I want to make sure you're okay."

Anna lasted a couple of months. Then Jess after her. Now Dana. They all pulled that same shit.

It's easy to get laid when people feel sorry for you.

7 · Lucy

When I get home from the movies, Mom's at the kitchen table with a cup of tea. She glances at the clock on the stove and sighs.

"You're late," she says. "It's 12:15."

"Yeah," I mumble, "it is." I don't tell her why I'm late. I don't explain that we actually pulled into the driveway at 12:03, but I had to listen to Hannah go on and on about Dustin and how sweet he is and how they like the same music and even though he's a little on the dumb side, it's not like she's looking to get married, so why not?

"I'm glad that you and Hannah have gotten so close in such a short period of time," Mom says, but her lips pinch together. "That doesn't mean you can miss curfew."

"I didn't mean to." I turn to get a glass from the cabinet and flip on the tap. "I tried."

"Try harder, sweetie. We worry about you, you know."

I nod. I know. I know it was hard for them, too; that it's hard for them to see how Trixie's parents have had to deal with losing a daughter.

"Did you have fun? You missed a wonderful dinner with the Stanfords."

I turn in surprise, glass in hand, water running in the sink behind me. "You made it home in time for dinner?" She usually closes on Saturday nights.

"It was important to Betty and Ron that I meet the people who will be living there all summer. I can only imagine how difficult it must be to leave your home in the hands of strangers, even though Shay is a friend of Betty's niece."

I turn back to the sink and fill my glass as she rehashes their conversations, tells me what Betty served, how Ron's Great Dane, Oscar, sat with his head on Simon's lap the entire time.

"Simon's adorable," Mom says as she gets up from the table, rinses out her cup, and puts it in the dishwasher. "He seemed very interested in you, Lucy. He asked a lot of questions." She smiles and tugs at a loose strand of my hair.

Before I get a chance to ask her what kinds of questions, she turns to straighten a dish towel hanging on the handle of the oven door and says, "I've got to get to bed. Don't stay up too late, okay, Luce?"

She goes upstairs, and I sit down at the table to finish my water.

My phone buzzes—Hannah always texts when she gets home so I know she's made it safely. I flip the phone over, but it's a number I don't recognize.

Sorry so late. This is Simon. Hope u don't mind ur mom gave me ur number. Can't wait to spend the summer on ur beautiful lake.

As much as I'm not happy that my mom thinks she can freely give out my number, my mouth turns up in a small smile as I think of something to text back. I'm not good at this. Trixie was the one who always knew what to say, and Hannah is, too. I've always been the shy one, the one who thinks things through a hundred times before making a decision.

My fingers hover over the screen. *See you soon*, I finally type.

Maybe this summer won't be so bad after all.

8 · Ben

I PULL INTO DANA'S DRIVEWAY, AND SHE SAYS, "I LOVE YOU, Ben."

I've told her that I love her a few times, but the words are hollow, untrue. Tonight I can't bring myself to say it. I walk her to the door in silence, then kiss her.

"Good night," I say, but I can't look her in the eye and see her sympathy. I don't deserve it.

I drive to Sullivan Street Park. It's closed, but I duck through the metal bars of the gate, like we used to do when we were kids. This is the best swimming spot in Halcyon Lake. Always has been. Always will be, no matter what happened here. I pull off my T-shirt and jeans and wade into the water.

Shit. It's cold.

I'll swim out to the island and back. That's it. One time. Three minutes out, three minutes back.

That's all it would have taken Trixie. Probably less. She could kick my ass in the water; she was such a strong swimmer. But it wasn't the water that took her, it was her heart. Abnormal electrical activity that caused sudden cardiac arrest. They said she'd probably had a heart condition her whole life and we never knew.

I've thought about that day a thousand times. How it might have been different.

If I'd raced with Trixie and Clayton to the island . . . If I'd already been in the water, I could have gotten to her sooner.

If they hadn't raced at all. If she'd been on the float.

If Lucy hadn't been there. If I'd been paying more attention.

If I hadn't been so enamored by Lucy's caramel-colored hair, tucked into a ponytail, strands of it loose and damp against the back of her soft, pale neck.

They tell me that nothing would have changed what happened. That nothing I would have done could have saved her.

That doesn't stop me from thinking about it until all the *ifs* twist themselves into a tight knot and burrow deep into my skin.

I swim in the ice-cold water, out to the island and back, over and over, until my entire body is numb and my own heart feels like it might stop. When I can't move another muscle, I lie on my back on a picnic table, reach up to the stars with one hand.

In this great, vast universe, I am nothing.

9 · Lucy

I wake up late Sunday morning, Mother's Day, to a quiet house. Dad's on the porch with a cup of coffee and the local paper.

"Where's Mom?" I ask. "Aren't we taking her out for lunch?"

He doesn't look up. "Nope. She's at the restaurant. Someone called in sick. She wants to know if you'll go in early."

I pinch my lips together. "I sort of had plans—uh, before my shift."

He puts his index finger on the newspaper to hold his place and looks up at me. "What kind of plans?"

"Well, I thought I'd stop at the cemetery for a few minutes."

He gives me a look that's a cross between worried and resigned. "Why are you always going up there, Luce?" His voice is soft, so quiet I have to strain to hear.

"I go once a month, Dad, not *always*. I miss her, okay?" The words rush out of me.

I used to go *always*. I used to go every day. Sometimes twice a day those first few weeks.

"Does it help?" he asks.

No, it doesn't help. Not really.

When I don't answer, he says, "I'll give you a lift when you're ready."

• • •

41

On the way to town, Dad doesn't let up. "I wish you'd get some new friends, Lucy."

"I have friends, Dad. Hannah is my friend."

"She's too loud."

I roll my eyes and change the subject. "So why did you tell Shay Stanford she could work down at our patio?"

Dad shrugs. "I worked out a deal with Ron and Betty. Fifty bucks a week. We could use the extra cash."

My stomach flips—I hate talking about money. I look at my dad. He needs a shave, his cheeks are hollow and there are dark circles under his eyes. He works at a plant that manufactures aluminum docks and boat lifts, but our lift sits empty. He sold the boat months ago, even though he's been working double shifts and overtime. My uncle Daniel says we can borrow his boat anytime, but I can't remember the last time Dad got out on the lake. Clayton's tuition is expensive; costs of restaurant supplies have shot up. I know money's tight.

When I don't say anything, he continues. "You'll be so busy this summer, you probably won't even notice."

Dad drops me off at the church. As he drives away my cell phone rings—the James Bond theme song. Clay.

"Hey," he says.

"How's the studying going?" I ask.

"Studying. Right. Good." He sounds ragged and rough, like he's got ashes in his mouth.

"Are you hungover? It's two in the afternoon!"

He laughs. "Maybe a little bit."

"I thought you were coming home for Mother's Day. Guess you had a change of plans?"

"Yeah. I have a final Monday morning, so, you know, I've got to study."

"Doesn't sound like you were studying last night."

Clayton laughs. "Oh, I was studying. Studying the Bud Light and the bootay."

Seriously?

"Hey, did you know that Ron and Betty rented out their house this summer—"

Clayton interrupts. "Yeah, yeah, Dad told me. Listen, you gotta do me a favor. You gotta tell Mom and Dad that I'm not coming home this summer."

"What?"

"Yeah, me and a couple of buddies are subleasing this guy's house. Total party house. Just for the summer."

"Since when?"

"Since a few days ago."

"I'm pretty sure Mom's counting on you to help out at the restaurant."

"Yeah, that's not gonna happen. Besides, I sort of have to do some makeup work for this class I screwed up in, so I figured I would get caught up and party, too. Best of both worlds."

"Best of both worlds for you, maybe."

"What's the big deal? Why do you care if I come home or not?"

"I don't. It's just—" But I do care. Everything's different.

Trixie's gone, Ben's gone, my first summer without them. No Betty and Ron, no pans of brownies and plates of peanut butter cookies. I can't be without Clay, too. I can't have any more *different*. I take a deep breath.

"You'll be fine, Lucy. You'll tell them for me, right?"

"Why should I?"

"Come on, help me out. I want to have fun this summer. I don't want to work at the restaurant."

"Oh, it's fine for me but not for you?"

"That's right. Looking out for number one."

"As usual," I spit. "Tell them yourself."

I pull the phone away from my ear and hit *end* as I walk across the cemetery.

Trixie's grave is on the side farthest from the church, close to a small cluster of silver maple trees. Her headstone is red granite, small and simple. Her name, the dates, *Beloved Daughter and Sister.*

Trixie's mother, Jane, has planted flowers, the earth damp where it's recently been watered. She's been here today. This is her first Mother's Day without Trixie.

At the foot of Trixie's grave is a small stone bench with cherubs carved into the legs. I sit and face the headstone.

"Hey, Trix." That's how I always begin.

And then I talk.

I talk about Emily and how excited I am to be her nanny this summer, even though I'm not all that excited about cleaning the cabins and hauling trash around. I tell her about my phone call with Clay, about Hannah and Dustin and the movie last night and how it still feels weird to go to the movies without her.

I tell her about the Clarks and the renters and Simon and his Dr Pepper T-shirt. "And, um, he's pretty cute," I say. "What do you think? Should I go for it with Simon the Renter?"

I move from the bench to kneel close to the headstone. I stroke my fingers over the tops of the marigolds.

"I've been seeing Ben around a lot lately. I'm worried about him, Trix. He's always so angry. He won't talk to me. I mean . . . I know it's hard for him without you. I get that. He misses you. But what I don't understand is why he had to take it out on me. Why did he push me away? Why did he say those terrible things?"

Trixie doesn't answer.

Only one person can answer those questions.

"I'm trying to be brave, Trixie," I whisper. "It was a lot easier when you were around to remind me."

I stand and brush grass from my knees. I reach into my pocket for a root beer barrel, twist the cellophane wrapper open, and place it on top of Trixie's headstone. I leave her a piece of candy from Sweet Pea's every time I visit, and every time I come back, it's gone. Root beer barrels, cinnamon disks, butterscotches, jawbreakers. All her favorites. I like to think she's enjoying the candy, even though it's probably taken by a raccoon or squirrel.

"I'm going to ask him," I say. "The next time I see him, I'm going to walk right up to him and ask him why he pushed me out of his life." I bring two fingers to my lips and then touch them to the top of the gravestone. "Later, Trix. I miss you."

I turn. My breath catches when I see Ben standing on the front steps of the church, leaning over the railing. He's watching me and he looks so sad. I wonder how long he's been there and if he could have possibly heard anything I said to Trixie.

I drop my eyes and walk down to the street. My brilliant plan to confront him, to get my answers, is crushed into the grass beneath every footfall.

10 · Ben

<small>Lucy's at the cemetery.</small>

It's Mother's Day, Mum's first without Trixie. I stopped going to church after Trixie died, and I never go to the cemetery, but this morning when Mum asked me to go, I didn't have the heart to say no. And it was bad. Mum cried and Dad hugged her and I sort of hung back at the edge of the row of headstones and let them have their moment.

She's not there. Trixie *died*, and what we put in the ground is a shell of what she was. I don't go into her room, and I can't bring myself to sit at her grave.

What good would it do? It wouldn't make me feel better.

Mum's been crying most of the day, so when Dad asked me to run back up here and bring her some lilacs from a bush at Trixie's grave, I went.

But Lucy's here.

I stand on the front steps of the church and I watch her. She's talking, but she's too far away for me to hear. She stands up and pulls something out of her pocket and places it on top of the gravestone. She kisses her fingers and presses them to the stone. I try to swallow the lump that's suddenly in my throat. I shouldn't be watching this.

Before I can move off the steps, though, Lucy turns and sees me.

Oh God, please don't let her walk over here and talk to me

now. I don't think I'll be able to keep it together. She must feel the same way, because she puts her head down and scurries away, fast.

I hate this. I hate that I can't figure out a way to make things better. I hate that I don't deserve to be forgiven.

I walk over to Trixie's grave and pull Mum's garden shears out of my back pocket. I've got to make this quick.

There's a root beer barrel on the stone. Trix and Lucy loved going to Sweet Pea's on Saturday mornings to spend their allowance money on candy. They'd come home and sit in the sunroom to divide up the bag—hard candy for Trixie, chocolate and fudge for Lulu.

Once, a few summers ago, I followed them to Sweet Pea's, made it seem like I was running an errand for Dad to the hardware store.

"Why are you following us, Ben?" Trixie asked.

"I'm not," I said, slowing my bike so that I didn't run into them.

"You're not supposed to ride your bike on the sidewalk," she said.

"Who's going to stop me?"

"Go home."

"I've got to pick up some nails for Dad."

"Nails?" Trixie cried. "What does he need nails for?"

"Dunno. He said for me to pick up some two-and-a-half-inch siding nails." I thought that sounded believable enough. "So that's what I'm doing. What are you doing?"

"You know what we're doing," Trixie said. "We're going to

Sweet Pea's." She stopped and turned around, her hands on' her hips. Lucy stopped, too, her hands jammed in the pockets of her shorts. She stared at the ground, didn't look up at me.

"Why don't you ever buy me any fudge, Lulu?" I asked. Her head snapped up, and her eyes were wide with something— surprise, fear, I didn't know. "Hey," I said, "I'm only teasing."

She blushed and turned away, started walking again.

"Leave us alone, Ben," Trixie said. "Go buy your nails."

Later, after Lucy had gone home, I found a piece of maple fudge, my favorite, wrapped in pea green tissue, on the desk in my bedroom next to my rock tumbler.

After that, every time the girls went to Sweet Pea's, I found a piece of maple fudge on my desk later. For two years. Until Trixie died and there were no more trips to Sweet Pea's, no more sounds of laughter from the sunroom.

I try not to cry as I cut a few blooms off the lilac bush, but I can't help it. I brush the tears away with the back of my hand before I walk back down the hill.

I was right to avoid this place. I won't come back here again.

the tallest tower in all the land

Trixie and Lulu loved to explore their world. They hiked in the woods and swam in the lakes. They caught fish and threw them back for another day.

They climbed trees in the park, giant box elder and oak, even though Lulu's heart raced with fear as she searched for footholds and held on with sweating palms. "Be brave," Trixie reminded her, and Lulu was. When she could go no farther, she looked out over the beautiful, tranquil lake for which their town was named: Halcyon. She had never seen anything so stunning. From here, at the top of this box elder tree, the lake was theirs. It belonged to them.

And then one day, Trixie's brother, Ben, told them he knew of a place with an even more spectacular view, the tallest tower in all the land. The entire countryside laid out before them—sky and cloud, lake and pine—for as far as the eye could see.

Lulu wondered if she would ever be able to climb such a tower, or if her fear would keep her away.

But one day, when Trixie was feeling particularly adventurous, the two best friends left behind their serene lake in search of the new and the unexplored, the promise of something they'd never before beheld.

If Lulu had been afraid of climbing the giant box elder tree in the park, she was paralyzed with fear when they finally reached their destination that perfectly cloudless summer *afternoon. The blue sky stretched out above them, and when Lulu tipped her head up and saw the giant wooden structure before her, her knees began to shake.*

"How tall is it?" Lulu asked.

Trixie did not know, exactly, but Ben had told her that there were one hundred and thirty winding steps to the top. "Lulu," Trixie said, "I know that deep inside, you have the courage to climb to the top of that tower."

So Lulu closed her eyes, and she reached down deep to the place inside her soul where she kept her most guarded reserve of courage, the one she relied on when she was most in need but kept protected because she did not want to use it all up at once. She began to climb.

And the climb terrified Lulu in ways she could not have imagined. She had felt dizziness before, but this sensation—the sky spun, the tower itself swayed—rocked her to the core. Many times, Lulu and Trixie paused so that Lulu could place both hands on the wooden railing, close her eyes, and wait for the world to come to a halt.

"We're almost there," Trixie said in a tender voice. "You'll be glad for it."

They climbed and rested and climbed again for what seemed like hours.

Finally, Trixie and Lulu reached the top of the tower. Lulu's balance returned and her stomach stopped its relentless lurching.

And the view, as Ben had promised, was spectacular.

In every direction, their world had no end. They looked

across the tops of pine and oak and maple, of birch and aspen and willow, to the myriad lake and river and pond, all glimmering in the summer sunlight. The sight took their breath away.

Lulu turned to her best friend. "This is the most amazing thing I've ever seen," she said.

Then Lulu glanced to the floor of the platform, which was covered with fragrant creeping thyme. Before her very eyes, the purple flowers multiplied and swirled around her feet, the end of a trail that tumbled down the stairs, all the way to the ground.

"Trixie, look!" Lulu cried. "Where did it come from?"

Trixie smiled. "From you, from your footsteps." She reached out and squeezed Lulu's hand.

The friends gazed upon their world a bit longer until the sun dipped below the trees to the west. They began their climb down through the cover of thyme, but Lulu was not as terrified as she had been going up.

When they reached the safety of the firm, solid earth, Trixie looked at her best friend with a smile and said, "Always remember that the thrill of the view is worth the terror of the climb."

Lulu would remember those words for the rest of her life.

JUNE

Silences make the real conversations between friends.
Not the saying, but the never needing to say that counts.
—*Margaret Lee Runbeck*

11 · Lucy

It's the first week of summer break.

Emily and I are playing on the resort's small playset. From here, I have a clear view of Ben as he works. He helps guests with their luggage and fishing gear, gives tours of the resort. He stands with his hands in his pockets and scowls as he watches a guest back a giant SUV and pontoon down into the boat launch—badly.

"Do you want to go to the library?" I ask Emily, pushing her so high on the swing that she squeals. Ben looks over and I duck my head down.

"No," she says. "You promised to teach me cartwheels."

It's such a beautiful early summer day that I don't blame her for not wanting to be inside. We move to a grassy spot closer to the lake.

"Do one," Emily says.

It's been months since I've set foot in the gym, but I lift my hands in the air and go over easily. The ground here is uneven and I stumble a bit on my landing. When I look up, I see Ben watching me from across the beach. I quickly turn away.

"Here," I say to Emily, my voice shaking, "you need to start small. Little jumps." I show her where to place her hands on the ground and how to hop from side to side. It will be a while before she'll be able to flip.

She flops down in the grass after a few hops. "Whew! That's hard work."

"Keep practicing and you'll get it." I do another cartwheel, then a roundoff. It feels familiar, freeing. I miss gymnastics. I miss movement. I feel like I've been standing still for months.

I sit down next to Emily. The grass is warm from the sun.

"Why don't you like Ben?" she asks.

The question comes out of nowhere and socks me in the stomach. "What makes you think I don't like Ben?" I almost choke on the words.

"You never talk to him. You don't laugh with him or tell him stories like you tell my mom and me. Why can't you be friends with him? You were friends with Trixie."

I nod and blink back the tears that, like Emily's question, have come out of nowhere. "Well, Ben and I used to be friends. We were all friends."

"But Trixie's in heaven now."

I nod again. I'm not prepared for this conversation.

"You aren't friends with Ben because Trixie's not here anymore? I don't get it."

That about sums it up. I don't get it, either.

"Well, Emily, it's not that Ben and I aren't friends, exactly." A tight ball of pain in my chest moves its way up into my throat. "It's—it's complicated."

"What's complicated mean?"

I pause again and pull at a blade of grass. "Complicated is like a puzzle. All the pieces have to fit a certain way, and it's tricky to figure out which pieces go where."

"Oh," she says, but I'm not sure that I've explained it well enough. "You know what I do when I'm working on a puzzle I can't figure out?"

"What do you do?"

"I ask my mom for help." Emily bounds up and runs back toward the swings.

That night, I don't sleep much. I wish I had the Book of Quotes. I wonder if Jane has cleaned out Trixie's room or if it's how we left it the morning we hurried to the park with our beach towels and sunscreen. I wonder if the notebook is on Trixie's desk where we'd set it the night before. She'd written a new quote from Audrey Hepburn: *The best thing to hold onto in life is each other.*

I open my laptop and create a new folder on my online bulletin board. I search for the quote and find a graphic of the words, handwritten in dark blue ink, swirling letters with doodles of hearts. It's perfect.

I search for more images: *growing up, best friends, memories.* I pin a dozen more quotes, some familiar, some new, and then find this Dr. Seuss quote: *Sometimes you will never know the value of a moment, until it becomes a memory.* I think about the moment I told Trixie that I had a crush on her brother, a bitter cold winter afternoon. We were twelve.

We were playing the Game of Life in Trixie's basement next to the woodstove, filling our plastic cars with pastel plastic babies. We always named our husbands after our latest crushes. For a long time I'd wanted to name my plastic husband Ben, but I was too shy and embarrassed and scared of what Trixie might think. I usually chose the most popular boy in class—a tall boy named Jack who all the girls liked—or Tyler Clark, my neighbor who was in high school.

"Congratulations!" Trixie said as she handed me a blue stick person. "I now pronounce you husband and wife. Who will it be this time? Jack? Tyler?"

I cleared my throat and took a deep breath. "Ben."

Trixie jumped up. "What?!" She spun around and twirled and clapped her hands. "Oh, this is perfect."

"Trix," I mumbled and tucked my chin down. My cheeks grew hot.

"Oh, you'll get married and have *lots and lots* of babies and the best part is that we'll be *sisters*, Lulu. *Sisters*."

I had been so worried that she would make fun of me or be mad or jealous. But I shouldn't have worried. This was Trixie, my sweet, caring, compassionate best friend.

She sat back down, and I twirled the spinner, my new pinhead husband named Ben next to me in the boxy pink car.

"What do you like best about him?" she asked.

"Come on, Trixie."

"Please? Five things?"

I named the first five things that came to mind: his one dimple that appeared when he laughed really hard. The gentle way he polished and handled his agate collection. That he called his mother "Mum" (at which point, Trixie interrupted with, "Wait a minute! I call her Mum, too!"). How adorable he looked when he held Emily. That whenever he was around, especially when we were out on the boat or swimming, I felt safe. I knew that no matter what, he would take care of me.

It would be three years before anything happened with Ben—before I thought that maybe he liked me, too—and all the while, I quietly loved him. We spent time together, the four of us—me and Clayton, Ben and Trixie—and we spent time apart. We grew up. I bought him fudge almost every week and left it in his room, even though he never mentioned it, never thanked me. I watched while he took other girls to football games and the movies, held their hands and kissed them at their lockers.

And Trixie was right by my side when I felt sad and inadequate and ugly, telling me that her brother was stupid and someday would realize how much he loved me.

I've been pinning quotes for a long time and I've got a crick in my neck. I reach up one hand to rub away some of the tension. I find one last quote: *It's a good day to have a good day*, swirling script over a photo of a lake.

Trixie was wrong.

12 · *Ben*

DANA WANTED TO GO TO THE MOVIES TONIGHT. WE SEE EVERY damn movie that comes to town. There's got to be something else we could do. We could drive over to Cloud 9, the campground outside of town, and play some mini-golf or hit the Lazy River. We could hike up to the Fire Tower and drink beer high above the treetops. We could go out on the boat, have a bonfire at Guthrie's. Anything but sit in that stifling, musty movie theater again.

I lied and told Dana I needed to stay home to help my dad tonight, but I don't think she bought it.

After dinner, I head upstairs to my room and flop down on the bed. I stand up and pace, I go to the window and watch the summer world of Halcyon Lake drift by.

Drifting.

I turn away from the window and bang my leg into the corner of my desk. The desk where Lucy used to leave fudge for me. The desk is covered with stones and equipment—agates, a rock tumbler, sandpaper, a shallow dish with white, chalky rings of evaporated water. All this stuff used to be my dad's, and I was so proud when he said I was old enough for it. That was fourth grade. I wanted to be like him—the fishing, the rocks. For a while I even thought I'd teach earth science, too.

I pick up an agate from a small pile on the desk. An

agate in the rough—one I'd found on a beach up the North Shore Scenic Drive along Lake Superior last summer but haven't polished. It's coarse and uneven and pitted on one side, so different from the beautiful striping and colors of the opposite side. It's got a lot of potential. They say it's worth more this way, uncut, in its natural state, but I've always liked the shine and design of the polished stones, the cabochons.

I gave Lucy an agate on that North Shore trip. I wonder if she kept it or if she tossed it aside, put it in a box of sentimental garbage. Years from now she'll pull the box out from under her bed, covered with dust, and wonder about the agate, where it came from.

I used to have the patience for polishing stones. I used to want to make something smooth and dynamic out of something dull and misshapen, but I haven't worked on any rocks since Trixie died. I've left everything the way it was, like Mum has left Trixie's bedroom.

I balance a few rocks into a small stack, careful to keep it from tumbling over. It reminds me of an inuksuk. Dad told us about them on our first trip to Duluth years ago when we saw a couple along the side of the road. They're stone structures that the Inuit used as guideposts, to mark good hunting or fishing, to give direction—practical reasons, but spiritual ones, too, Dad said, as memorials or to mark a place of respect. Last summer, that last trip before Trixie died, we saw at least fifty of them at one of the rocky beaches.

My tower is irregular, off balance, but the clink of the stones as I stack them is like a balm on my soul. I've created something.

But unlike an inuksuk, these rocks don't tell me which direction to go.

I sweep my hand across the stack and the stones crash to the desk.

13 · Lucy

MONDAY, MY DAY OFF. I SLEEP IN, THEN THROW ON SHORTS and a ratty Halcyon Lake Hawks hockey T-shirt, and get to work cleaning the house, something that falls on me a lot more now that Mom and Dad are both working longer hours. I've got a pretty good routine down, starting at the loft at the top of our log home and working my way down, the kitchen last.

I've just finished vacuuming the living room when I look through the sliding glass door and see Shay Stanford down at the lake. She and Simon have been here a couple of days. Simon and I have texted a few times, but I haven't been home much, and I'm nervous about seeing him again. Nervous and excited.

Shay stands with her hands on her hips, looking out over the lake, the sunlight a bright, rippling streak across the water. The trees are starting to fill out in a brilliant green, and the air is thick with the scent of lilac and lily of the valley.

Any other time, I'd stop what I was doing and walk down to take it in, to sit in my favorite chair on the patio and let myself get lost in the cool, fresh breeze.

I can't do that now. Shay has set up her easel and sketch pads and what looks like a tackle box, the cover open, art supplies spilling across the table. When she turns back from the lake, the smile on her face is wide and as bright as the sunlight on the water.

That's got to be worth more than fifty bucks a week.

I open up the bank of living room windows, make a quick round of the bookshelves and tables with a dust rag, and move on to the kitchen.

The kitchen doesn't see a lot of use these days, not with Mom at the restaurant all the time. It doesn't take long for me to load and start the dishwasher, wipe down the countertops, and go through the stack of mail. When I'm finished, I take a glass of water out to the deck, lean over the railing, and watch Shay again. I wonder where Simon is, what he's doing.

I don't have to wonder very long. When I turn to go back into the house a few minutes later, Simon Stanford is standing at the fireplace, a framed photograph in his hand.

He's here. My heart jumps a little, but my glance quickly moves to the mantel above the fireplace. I know the exact photo he's taken down.

The four of us—me and Clay, Ben and Trixie—on the dock in front of the Porters' pontoon, two months before Trixie died. Ben stands in between me and Trixie, his arms over our shoulders. He's wearing jeans and a green T-shirt. But he's not looking in the direction of the camera. He's looking at me.

It's my favorite picture of all of us.

The last picture.

"Put that down," I snap, and I walk across the room and snatch the frame out of Simon's hands.

He takes a step back, his hands in the air. "Whoa, sorry. I rang the bell. You didn't answer, but the door was open, and I could see you out on the deck." He grins.

"So why didn't you come out to the deck, then? You had to snoop around?"

"I wasn't snooping around, Lucy. This is a great picture of you. Who are the others?" He steps around so he's standing next to me to look at the photo again. He taps the glass. "This guy must be your brother—looks just like you. Who's the other one? Your boyfriend?"

I step away from him, set the photo back in its place on the mantel, and swallow hard.

"No." I turn back around to face him. "He's not my boyfriend, not that it's any of your business."

Simon doesn't react the way I expect him to: He laughs. Then he says, "Lucy, I'm sorry. I guess I should have found a less intrusive way to find out if you have a boyfriend. My reasons for asking are purely selfish, of course."

My anger dissolves in an instant. My cheeks go red, and I tuck my chin. When I look up again seconds later, Simon is grinning at me.

"So," he says, "what should we do today? I'm dying of boredom over there and you're finally home. Any chance you could show me around town?"

I look down at my filthy clothes and take a surreptitious sniff—sweat and the pungent pine of floor cleaner. I'm fairly certain there's a streak of dirt across one cheek. My phone chimes as I reach up a hand to rub away the dirt.

"Hold that thought," I say, grateful for the chance to step

away and think about my answer as that queasy nervous feeling swirls through me again.

The text is from Daniel. *Jeannie's home with a sick kid. Please can you work 3–6 until Rosemary comes in?*

I glance at the time. It's 1:15 now. By the time I shower and change, it will be almost two, and then I'll need to walk to town. Hannah's in Texas with her mother for the book tour, Dad's at work, and it's doubtful that anyone from the Full Loon would be able to get away to pick me up.

"That was my uncle," I tell him. "I help out at our family restaurant, and they need me to come in. Could you give me a ride to town, and I'll show you around another time?"

He frowns. "How late do you have to work?"

"Until six."

"Okay, six is another time. I'll drive you to work and meet you there when your shift is over."

He smiles at me, quick and wide and genuine. Sparks ignite in my chest. I blush and stare at the Captain America symbol on his heather gray T-shirt.

"Thanks," I mutter to the white star on his shirt. "I'll be in the driveway at 2:30."

The minute I walk in the door, Mom gets on my case for being an hour late.

"What are you talking about?" I ask. "Daniel asked me to work from three to six."

"No," Mom says, "*two* to six."

I open the message and shove my phone in her direction. She glances down and passes it back.

"Well, get your apron on and take over the front tables."

"You're welcome," I mutter under my breath.

Later, my shift almost over, Clare catches me as I walk past. "Thanks for coming in on your day off, Lucy. We would have been in the weeds without you."

"Thanks," I say. "I'm glad somebody around here appreciates my help."

Clare's a hostess here and Daniel's girlfriend. They live together in an apartment above the Goldilocks hair salon, where she also works part time.

"Give your poor mom some slack, Luce. It's been a hard couple of months since Rita left. I'm working longer days, too, but I can't do much more, not with my hours at the salon."

"So replace Rita already."

"You know better than anybody how hard that can be. You've seen the parade of waitstaff we've had come through here the last five years. Your mom wants someone dependable, who's in it for the long haul. That takes time."

"Six weeks?"

Clare doesn't get a chance to respond because the red screen door opens and closes with a bang, and Ben Porter walks in.

Oh, God. It's Monday night. Why did I ever agree to work on a Monday night? Ben and Guthrie have been coming here every Monday night since right after Trixie died.

I scurry behind the counter before he makes it to the hostess stand. From here, I'm blocked by a partition but can still hear every word.

"Hey, Ben," Clare says. "I saved you a table."

Please don't let it be one of mine.

"Thanks," he says, "but I'll just eat at the counter. I'm on my own tonight."

My first thought is one of relief since I don't have the counter tonight, but then I realize that I'm standing behind it. I push my way through the swinging door into the kitchen but not before Ben slides onto the stool at the far end of the counter. I'm sure he saw me.

I press myself against the wall and take a few deep breaths.

"Whoa," Daniel says. "You look like you've seen a zombie."

"You might say that," I say in a quiet voice, not that Ben would be able to hear me over the din of the café and the noise Daniel and Chris, another cook, are making back here.

"Ben's here, huh? He's early."

Daniel's a lanky guy with a mess of dark hair, a scruffy goatee, and a fondness for classic rock. Today he's wearing a Blue Öyster Cult T-shirt. He's only ten years older than me, more like another older brother than an uncle.

"Remind me never to work on a Monday again," I tell him. I finally feel like I'm starting to catch my breath.

"Wanna take his burger out to him?"

"Very funny."

"All right, if you won't do that, the order for eleven is up."

I load the plates on a tray and back out of the kitchen, pivoting so that I can't see Ben at the end of the counter.

I make it through the next fifteen minutes, although there are times when I feel Ben's eyes on me. I finish up my last table and pass the rest on to Rosemary. I'm untying my apron when Simon walks through the door.

Simon—I'd forgotten about Simon.

He's asking for a table for two.

"There you are!" He pulls me into a hug. In front of everyone at the Full Loon Café. My mother, Clare, even Daniel, who is at the counter talking to Ben.

And Ben.

I pull away.

"You know Lucy?" Clare asks Simon.

"Of course I know Lucy," he says much too loudly. "My family's renting the Clarks' house this summer."

"Oh, sure, you're one of the renters." Clare sets menus down on the table.

I sit down and when I glance up again, I notice that we're in Ben's direct line of vision. I can see him and he can see me. Us.

"Why did you ask for a table, Simon?" I ask after Clare has gone back to the hostess stand.

"Mrs. Clark said the pie is really good here. What would you recommend?"

"Baked pie or cream pie? Fruit? Candy?" I slip into my waitress mode. Daniel's pie is the best around.

"Not fruit," he says. "It's *pie*."

"What? That's the *best* kind of pie. My favorite's strawberry rhubarb."

"Gross. How's the coconut cream?"

"You can't go wrong with the coconut cream."

Apparently Simon's not just here for the pie, because when Patty comes over to take our order, he asks for a half rack of ribs, a bowl of wild rice soup, and a slice of coconut cream.

Simon tells me about his school—an arts magnet—and the hardware store his dad and grandfather own. "Dad wants me to take over someday, but I don't want to be stuck at the store my whole life, you know what I mean?"

I nod. I do know what he means.

Mom brings over our order herself. "Simon, so wonderful to see you. And how nice that you and Lucy are having dinner together. Enjoy your meal. Compliments of the house." She winks at me. I roll my eyes.

I got a slice of Loonberry pie, a crazy mix of whatever berries Daniel has on hand with a crumble topping and a scoop of homemade vanilla ice cream. I watch Simon eat, half listen to him ramble on about the graphic novel he's writing. He's artistic like his mom.

And when I'm not watching Simon, I watch Ben. He pulls his phone out of his pocket, scowls, and taps on the screen with one thumb. He puts it facedown next to his plate and scrubs a hand over his face.

Was it a text from Guthrie? His mom? Dana?

I look away, press my fork into the last bits of berry on my plate.

Simon twists around in Ben's direction.

"Why do you keep looking back there? Do you know that guy at the counter or something?"

I nod. "Sort of."

"Just sort of?"

"Yeah, I know him. I guess you could say that we used to be friends."

"Used to be." It's not a question. He turns back around to get another look at Ben. "Old boyfriend?"

"No."

"You have a crush on him or something?"

"No," I say, probably too quickly, because Simon nods his head like he knows some big secret.

"Hey, that's the guy from the picture, isn't it? The one from your mantel? I totally get it now."

"No, I don't think you do." My words are sharp.

"Well, why don't you fill me in?"

I pause. Why should I tell him my problems?

"Come on, Lucy, don't be like that. You're the only person I know up here." He smiles, and his whole face lights up under all that shaggy hair.

With Ben sitting across the restaurant, it's hard to tell if I could like Simon. But he's nice. And cute. And he's sitting *right here*, eating a slice of coconut cream pie. No time like the present, Hannah would say.

"His name is Ben," I say in a low voice. "We used to be friends. I mean, his sister was my best friend, and then—well, Ben and I aren't friends anymore. He's—I don't know—we don't talk anymore."

"That's it?"

"It's a long story," I say. "Complicated. And it doesn't matter anymore."

"Okay." Simon grows quiet. After a minute he says, "What about his sister? Are you still friends with her?"

I swallow. "She died."

"Oh." He drags out the word. "I'm sorry."

"Like I said, it doesn't matter." The words rush out.

"If it didn't matter, you wouldn't be spending so much time looking over there," Simon says, his voice light.

"Trust me," I say. "It. Doesn't. Matter."

"Okay, okay. I believe you." He stands up and drops a few singles on the table. "Well, I'm ready for you to show me the town. Let's go for a drive."

I stand up. Simon holds out his hand and I hesitate.

"Take my hand," he whispers. "That will get your boy's undies in a bunch."

I can do this. I can. And it's just for show, right?

I link my fingers with his, warm and soft and strangely comforting. We walk through the restaurant, and Clare winks at me as we walk past.

I get into the front seat of Simon's car. As we drive out of the parking lot, it's all I can do to keep my head from swiveling around to see if Ben has come out of the café and is watching us drive away.

"Where to?" Simon asks.

We're headed north, out of town. "Keenan's Cloud 9 Vacationland," I say. "Take a right at the next stoplight."

"Cloud 9? Sounds euphoric."

"Oh, you have no idea. It's this 1950s-themed campground with a water park and an outdoor movie theater and mini-golf. It's impossible to not have a good time at Cloud 9."

"Sounds weird," he says.

I shake my head. "You're not allowed to dis Cloud 9. It's like walking onto the set of *Grease*. And maybe, if we're lucky, *Grease* will be playing at the amphitheater tonight, too."

Simon groans, but after we arrive, the smile doesn't leave his face. He insists on paying for our two-hour passes, and we weave our way through the crowd—lots of tourists and a few people I recognize from school. We head to Blueberry Hill, the mini-golf course.

"I'm absolutely terrible at this," Simon tells me as I hand him his club.

He is. There's no other word for it. I've played this course a thousand times and could make par with my eyes closed, but Simon knocks the ball onto the next green, into the stream, everywhere it's not supposed to go. At one point, we let the foursome behind us go ahead. But he laughs at himself, shakes his hair out of his eyes, and sings along (badly) to the fifties music at each hole.

We don't bother to add up our scores. We walk back down the hill toward the Snack Shack. He buys a bag of popcorn, and we sit on a bench near the amphitheater.

"That was fun," he says. "What's up next? A *Grease* sing-along?"

I reach into the pocket of my shorts for my phone to check the time and my fingers graze the agate.

I think about the way Ben glared at us at the restaurant.

I want so badly to move on, to just be a normal girl playing mini-golf with her date.

I'm not.

"I need to get home." I stand up and Simon does, too. I crumple up the greasy popcorn bag and toss it in the trash can next to the bench. "Long day tomorrow."

"Oh yeah, me too." He follows me as I walk toward the exit. "I mean, for starters, I'm planning to sleep until at least ten. Then I might hang out down by the lake."

"Sounds rough."

When we reach his car, Simon opens the passenger door for me. "I'd love to come back here with you sometime."

"Sure, we could float down the Lazy River."

"You must come here a lot."

I shake my head as I slide in. "Not as much as I used to."

I don't say anything else. He closes my door and gets in himself, and we're quiet for a few minutes as we drive out of the parking lot and back toward town.

"I'm really sorry about your friend," Simon says softly. "Was it—was it weird for you to be at Cloud 9 without her?"

"Yeah, a little. But it's okay. We don't have to talk about it."

I don't want him to feel sorry for me. I like that he doesn't know my history, the details about Trixie's death. I change the subject as we drive through town, and I give him the grand tour of Halcyon Lake. I point out the candy shop, the used bookstore, the hair salon and the apartments above.

"My uncle and his girlfriend live there," I say as we drive past. "Daniel's a cook at the diner and you met Clare—the hostess?"

I tell him about my family and Emily. I pause and hold my breath as we drive past Ben's house, his Firebird parked in front of the third door.

"The park," I say, and I wave my hand in that direction. "Sullivan Street Park. Great place for a picnic and the best swimming beach in town."

"Cool! When can we go?"

"Go?"

"Yeah, go swimming? At the park?"

I shake my head. "I'm not much of a swimmer."

"Really? You live on a lake."

"Yeah."

"But you don't like to swim?"

"Nope." Too many weeds, too much rocky sand under my feet, too much unknown in the murky lake. "I love to be out on the lake, though. In a sound, sturdy watercraft, of course."

He pulls into the Clarks' side of the driveway and walks me to my door, like this is a real date or something.

"I had a great time with you, Lucy."

For a second I think he's going to lean in and kiss me. He doesn't. His cheeks turn pink, and I wonder if he's thinking about it, too.

"It was fun," I say.

It's the truth. I had fun with him. I smile up at him and he grins back.

"See you soon," he says, and walks across the driveway.

When he's almost out of sight behind Betty's gigantic lilac bush, he turns and holds his hand up in a wave.

I wave, too, and then slip my hand into my pocket. The agate is still there, safe.

14 · Ben

HE'S HOLDING HER HAND, FOR FUCK'S SAKE. LIKE IT'S A DATE or something. I watch them walk out of the café, throw some bills down on the counter, wait until the count of thirty, and follow them.

Lucy and the dickhead who drives a Volvo.

It's crazy, I know. Lucy working at the resort for the summer is driving me crazy. She's so close, right there, but I can't touch her, can't talk to her. Emily talks to me, wants to play with me, but Lucy sort of hangs back. Like she never wants to talk to me again. And that's nobody's fault but my own.

I'm careful to stay three or four cars behind so they don't notice. I'm trying to tell myself it's because I want to make sure she's safe, that this Simon guy isn't some psycho killer abducting her in his jackass Volvo. They head out the county road past the Fire Tower toward Stone's Throw Lake and turn in at Cloud 9.

That's when I realize how stupid I am.

What am I going to do? Follow them into the park? Walk through the crowds alone, spy on them when they buy ice cream at the Snack Shack and watch cartoons at the amphitheater?

Pathetic.

She's fine. She likes him.

She's over it. Me.

I fucked it up and she's moved on.

I whip the Firebird around toward home.

Dad's left the liquor cabinet open again. I take a bottle of whiskey up to my room. I'm going to sit here and stack rocks and drink until I get the picture of Lucy and that shaggy-haired jackass out of my head.

I'm late for work the next morning. I find my dad in the pole barn working on a motor, and he is pissed.

"Well?" he says without looking up from the workbench. "Where have you been?"

Where have I been, he wants to know.

"Well?" Dad says again when I don't answer him.

"I had something I needed to do."

What I needed to do was wake up puking, which caused a pretty significant delay.

He lets out a long breath. "You could have let one of us know. John had to take your guests out. They were tired of waiting. Now he's behind schedule."

Dad turns to look at me when I don't say anything. His hands and fingernails are dark with grease, the skin around his eyes grooved with deep wrinkles. We used to spend a lot of time together. We used to have a lot in common. You'd think that after Trixie died, we'd have grown closer, but lately I can't stand to be around him. And it's more than the drinking. He's always in a shitty mood.

Maybe we do have something in common.

"Ben, how many times have I told you? You have responsibilities now. People are counting on you. With employment come certain responsibilities."

He pauses, and it's all I can do to stop myself from mimicking him as he says the inevitable next words: "With *life* come certain responsibilities."

"You don't say." I can't keep the bitterness out of my tone.

"Don't get smart with me, Ben. I'm not in the mood for it."

I've heard that one before, too. He's a broken record. He teaches the same curriculum every year; he gives the same spiel out on the lake; he spews the same parental garbage.

It wasn't like this when Trixie was alive. We used to have real conversations. We talked about a lot of things—school and fishing and the Firebird. Or sometimes, like it is with Guthrie and me, we didn't talk. We sat out on the boat and fished and didn't have to say anything at all, and that was okay, too.

"Those two guys staying in Wolf?" Dad says. "They brought in a nice stringer of sunnies and just finished gutting them. You should probably clean the fish house."

I turn without a word and walk across the grass to the fish house. Shit. Nothing like cleaning up rotting fish guts in a shack on a hot morning when I could be out on the lake. Thank you, Lucy and the dickhead.

Later, after I've finished cleaning the fish house, I tell Tami that I feel like shit—not a lie—and am taking off the rest of the day. I need to walk, clear my head, so I hit the trail that winds along the edge of the lake from here to Sullivan Street Park. I'll come back for my car later.

The trail is quiet today—usually it's busy with joggers and

bikers and families looking for a quiet place to fish with their kids, away from the crowded park.

I'm about halfway to the park when I reach a group of trees that Trixie and I used to climb, years ago, when our parents first let us walk here by ourselves.

I look around and find a handful of rocks, most about the size of a softball, and I stack them near one of the tree trunks. The top stone topples and I start again, changing the order of the rocks until they're all balanced.

Satisfied, I hoist myself up into a crook of one of the trees. I lean against the trunk and reach into my pocket to switch off my phone.

I can't think of a better place to sleep off my hangover.

15 · Lucy

I DON'T SEE SIMON MUCH THE NEXT COUPLE OF DAYS AFTER our "date," and I do my best to avoid Ben at the resort. But on Saturday morning I walk into John and Tami's kitchen and he's there.

He's sitting at the table. It's late—he shouldn't be here. He should already be out on the lake or mowing the lawn or fixing a dock. Something. He lowers his head. I sit down next to Emily.

"Well," I say, "what's in store for today?"

"Boat!" she cries. "Let's go out in the boat. Can we, Daddy?"

"Sure," John says.

"Ben, would you mind taking them out?" Tami asks.

I'm not sure how the rest of the conversation goes, because all I hear is the roaring in my ears after Tami asks Ben to take us out fishing.

I don't want this. I don't want to spend the morning on a boat in the middle of the lake with Ben. This is the worst thing that could happen. I can't escape him when we're out on the lake together.

Tami sets a plate of bacon and scrambled eggs in front of me. "Eat something before you go out."

"We shouldn't bother Ben, Emily," I say, the words scratchy. "I don't want to keep him from his work."

"It's no *bother*." I'm surprised to hear Ben's voice. "I'll get the boat ready while you finish your breakfast."

Ben gets up so fast he almost knocks the chair over. I know that the boat's ready. It's always ready. He wants to get out of here, alone, before he has to suffer with me.

I take my time with breakfast while Emily finishes the red grapes on her plate. When I'm done, I get a washcloth from the bathroom and clean Emily's face and hands.

"You'll need your hair up so it doesn't blow in your face," I say, and she brings me her comb and a ponytail holder. Next we put on sunscreen. I drag the process out as long as possible, imagining Ben at the dock, doing whatever he needs to do as slowly as possible, too.

"You're so patient with her," Tami says as she loads the dishwasher. "No wonder she adores you so much, Lucy."

"Thanks," I say, but my face burns. If she only knew the real reason behind my patience today.

Emily declares herself ready. She has a bag with snacks—a juice box, fruit strips, and cheese crackers shaped like little birds—and two Fancy Nancy books. I grab my sunglasses and my phone, and we walk down the stone pathway to the dock.

My heart does its absurd little flutter when I catch sight of Ben standing on the dock talking to Tom, his dad. I've done a pretty good job of avoiding Tom this summer, too. He sees us, and I put my hand up in a tiny wave. Emily skips down the rest of the path and leaps into Ben's arms.

"Thank you for taking us out on the boat, Ben," she yells.

I catch up with her on the dock. Tom hands me a life vest and Ben fastens a small one on Emily.

"Hey there," Ben's dad says to me, "it's nice to see you." He doesn't call me Lulu.

I nod, but can't find my voice. I take a deep breath and step off the dock into the boat. I teeter a bit—it's been almost a year since I've gone out on the lake.

Ben reaches out and grabs my elbow to steady me, but I wrench my arm away.

"Please don't touch me," I whisper, but he's already crossed the boat to the driver's seat. I don't know if he heard me or not.

This is how I get through a miserable morning on the lake: I talk to Emily. Nonstop. If she isn't talking, I am. I begin by narrating our surroundings, which sets Emily off on a string of questions about trees and loons and fish and the weather that will easily occupy my time.

I love to be out on the lake. Between my dad's boat and the Porters', I spent much of my childhood summers fishing and sunning myself on the pontoon. I love everything about it—the bright sun reflecting off the water, the smell of fish and gasoline, wildflowers and weeds, sweet coconut sunscreen. I love the breeze that cools my baking skin, blows my hair back as we speed across the lake. The coolness of the water, murky with pondweed and coontail. The endless shoreline of jack pines and cabins and docks.

For a few minutes, I close my eyes, feel the warm morning sun on my face. I tip my head back and pretend that this is *before*. Trixie is here with us, and Clayton maybe, or Guthrie, and Ben is at the helm, like he is now, but it's the old Ben, before he became so angry and cold. It's my Ben.

"Lucy," Emily says, and I open my eyes. "How did Trixie die?"

My breath catches. Ben's head snaps up.

"Emily, I don't—I'm not sure that . . . today—" I can't think straight. I can't think of a way to talk about this, especially in front of Ben.

And then he's right next to her, taking her hand. "Hey," he says, and his voice cracks. "You know this. Trixie's heart was sick. She went for a swim and her heart stopped working."

He's so calm, so gentle, and I can't speak. I'm not ready for this. She's too young to really understand. But he told her enough.

Emily turns to me. "Is my heart sick? Will it stop working?"

"Oh, no," I say. I kneel in front of her and put my arms around her, even though now I'm right next to Ben. "You shouldn't worry about that, sweetheart. What happened to Trixie doesn't happen to everyone."

"Were you there, Lucy?" she says. She pulls away from me and looks at Ben. "Were you?"

I nod, but I don't look at Ben.

"Hey, I thought you wanted to catch some fish," he says, and thank God, it distracts her. Her face, so sad a minute before, breaks into a huge smile.

She grabs my hand and pulls me up from my crouching position. "You fish, too."

"No, that's okay," I say, and it's all I can do to hold back a sob.

"No!" she says with more force. "I want you to fish with me. Ben, tell her that you'll teach her how to fish."

Ben doesn't need to teach me how to fish. I knew how to bait a hook before I could write my own name.

"Okay, I'll fish with you," I say.

She scrambles up to a seat in the bow and swings her legs back and forth. To join her I have to pass very close to Ben. I hold my breath. When he steps up to the bow, he hands me a rod and reel and for the briefest second, his fingers touch mine. I don't mean to, but I jerk away like I've been shocked.

He doesn't move. He's so close. He must surely hear how loudly my heart pounds against my rib cage.

He leans toward me, and for a split second I have this insane thought that he is going to kiss me, right here, standing in the Crestliner in the middle of Halcyon Lake.

"Lucy?" he says in a low voice. "Are you okay?"

I nod. And then it's over. He looks away.

"I'll help Emily if you don't need me, then."

She squeals when he hands her a worm, bounces on her toes when her line gets a bite, and Ben helps her reel in a tiny bluegill.

I will always need him.

I sit in the bow and cast again and again, watch the bobber, wait for something. Anything.

16 · Ben

LATER THAT MORNING, AFTER I BRING LUCY AND EMILY BACK to shore, I find Tami in the garden, kneeling in a row of tomato plants.

"Hey," I say.

She looks up. "Hi."

"Listen, today was fine, but you know, I guess I'd rather not take Emily out on the boat anymore. Makes me nervous."

She lifts her hand to shield her eyes from the bright sun behind me. She must know I'm lying.

But Lucy almost broke me when she reached for my two-hundred-dollar rod and reel that I don't even let Guthrie use and then jerked away like I'd stung her.

"If you say so, Ben." Tami goes back to her vegetables.

I do. I say so.

I drive around for a while, not ready to go home. I rub my hand across the top of the steering wheel.

"Hey, beauty," I say. If there's one thing I can count on, it's my car. She's old but she hasn't failed me yet.

I bought the Firebird the spring before Trixie died, the spring of my sophomore year. I'd been sixteen for only a few weeks, but I'd been saving for months. This guy named Buck who went to high school with my dad was selling it, and even though he'd wanted to unload it before winter, he'd told me he'd wait until I had the money. I picked up a part-time gig doing maintenance at the arena and helped out John at the resort with occasional odd jobs.

The four of us—Dad, Mum, Trixie, and me—drove out to Buck's house on Iron Lake once I had the check. He lived way past Clayton and Lucy's, down a narrow one-lane gravel road on the peninsula. He handed me the keys on a water-stained leather fob, and I slid in and everything was right in the world.

"Her name is Brigitte," Buck said. He had a long gray ponytail and reeked of stale cigarettes. He leaned in, his arm across the top of the doorframe.

"Her?"

"Yeah. Brigitte. Named her after a girl I knew in college. Take good care of her, now."

"Will do," I said.

"And don't smoke in her. That was my only hard and fast rule. You gotta show the old girl some respect."

Trixie rode home with me. She put her feet up on the dash.

"Get your filthy flip-flops off my new car," I said, and swatted her leg.

"Don't you mean Brigitte?" she said. "That guy. What a weirdo."

"I don't know about weird. He works at the marina. He's decent. I mean, to hold onto her until I had the money, you know?"

"Seems like a waste to go to college and end up working at a marina," Trixie said. "I mean, I know that college is more than just your degree, but really?"

I thought about that for a while as we drove down County 5, Iron Lake on one side of us, Halcyon Lake on the other. Trixie had it all worked out. She'd go to school to become an elementary-school teacher, coach the swim team, someday have a family, but not before she'd lived in London with our gram for a year or two. She knew what she wanted out of life. Mum and Dad thought I should be a teacher, too. Summers off, Dad always said, can't beat that. But I couldn't see myself cooped up in a classroom for nine months of the year. I didn't want to teach, I wanted to fish. I needed to be outside.

"I don't know," I said. I was going to be a junior. My parents were after me for a decision—I'd already made one, I just hadn't told them. I wanted to go to the University of Minnesota up in Crookston and study natural resources. Water management. I told Trixie that day.

"Good for you," she'd said. "You don't always have to be what people expect you to be. Do what you love, Ben. Life is short, so live it. Be happy."

"Okay, okay. I get the picture."

She would have been a great teacher.

I don't call the Firebird Brigitte, but I see Buck around town once in a while. He always caresses her and tells her he still loves her. And I think about that day and how Trixie told me to be happy.

I would have been happy living in Halcyon Lake for the rest of my life, I think, if Trixie hadn't died. Maybe I would have started my own guide business. Maybe someday I would have taken over Apple Tree Lane. But Minnesota's full of lakes, everywhere you look. Northern Wisconsin, too. I can leave town, like Clayton did, walk away and not look back.

But not today. I pull into the arena parking lot and turn around toward home.

17 · Lucy

Sunday night, after my shift at the Full Loon, I ride home with my mom. Usually she doesn't stay much past seven on Sundays, but tonight she waited for me.

As soon as we're out of town, she says, "I'm sure you've heard I finally hired Rita's replacement."

"Yep."

"Her name is Joellen. She's married with a couple of kids. They live out on Papyrus Lake."

"That's nice."

"She can't work Monday nights during the summer, so I need you to pick up another shift."

Monday nights. Ben will be there.

"No." It's more of an exhale than a word.

"Look, Lucy, this isn't a request. I need you to do this."

"Can't you ask Jeannie to do it? Or Rosemary?"

"Rosemary works the day shift. And Jeannie's working five days."

"What about Patty? Or hire another part-timer."

She sighs. "Patty already works the Monday night shift. You know how hard it is to find good staff. Look how long it took me to find Joellen."

"Mom. I can't do it."

"Lucy, please. We're stretched pretty thin this summer as it is.

I can't hire another part-timer, especially when I had to hire someone to take Clayton's place."

I swallow hard and tell myself it's not just about Ben.

"Mom," I start, and my voice cracks. "It's my only day off. The only day I get any time to myself, you know? This summer—this summer has been so hard already . . ."

She sighs and there's a pause. Then, in that tender voice I've heard so much over the last ten months, she says, "It's been almost a year, sweetheart. I know that Trixie was a good friend, the best friend, and we all loved her, but at some point you have to let go of this sadness. It's time. It's time to move on, to get on with your life."

She reaches across the center console and squeezes my hand.

She doesn't understand. She doesn't, the counselors at school don't, the ones who said that it was okay to be sad, but we had to learn that life goes on, that we need to move on, carry on.

I hated them for saying it.

"No," I whisper into the window. Tears slip down my cheeks.

The car fills with a cloud of uncomfortable quiet that settles around us for the rest of the drive. When we get home, I run to the backyard to my escape, the lake. Shay won't be down there at this time of night.

But Simon is.

He's dragged two of the Adirondack chairs down to the beach. The sky is a dusky blue, not quite dark.

I'm surprised to see him here, but I'm not unhappy about it. He won't tell me that it's time to move on.

I wipe a hand across my cheeks to check for lingering tears. I sit down in the empty chair. "Hi," I say.

"Hey," he says. "Feels like I haven't seen you for days. I've missed you. Are you feeling better?"

Last night, after my morning out on the boat with Emily and Ben, I'd been exhausted. I ignored Simon's call and texted that I wasn't feeling well, and I wouldn't be able to go to the movies like we'd planned.

"Mm-hmm."

He takes a long drink from his glass. "Sun tea. Mom made it today. You want some?"

He offers me his glass, but I shake my head. His fingers are stained sky blue.

"I'm okay, thanks."

"How was work? I tried to talk Mom into having dinner at the Full Loon tonight, but she was too into her painting, you know? So I had a peanut butter sandwich instead." He laughs. "Doesn't compare."

"Were you painting today, too?" I point at his stained fingers.

"Oh, uh, yeah," he stammers. "I'm not as good as Mom, but yeah. I could show you sometime."

I nod, but don't say anything. I close my eyes and lean my head against the back of the chair.

"I like it up here," Simon says after a minute, "but I could never live in a place like this. It's too quiet."

"Too quiet?" I open my eyes and look at him. "How can it be *too* quiet?"

"In St. Paul, there's this constant stream of noise. The air is solid with it. Sirens. Music. Talking, shouting. It never stops, not even in the middle of the night." There's fondness in his voice.

"And you *like* that?"

"Yeah, it's like I know I can go to sleep because somebody else is always going to be awake, making sure that things go on as normal. I don't have to keep watch all the time."

"What are you keeping watch for?"

He shrugs. "You know it's just me and my mom, right? My parents have been divorced for a long time. Things weren't always great between them, you know? So I watch out for my mom, I guess."

"Where does your dad live?"

"South St. Paul, not too far from us."

"Shh. Don't talk for a minute," I say. "It's actually not that quiet."

I smile as I hear the cry of a loon overhead, the rustle of the leaves in the breeze, the chirp of an angry chipmunk, the rumble of a motor out on the lake.

"I stand corrected," he says. "How can you sleep with all this noise?"

"It's soothing," I tell him. "No matter what, life on the lake goes on."

"Lucy?"

"Yeah?"

"If I ask you something, will you be honest with me?"

I hesitate before I nod.

"Was, uh, was Ben your boyfriend?"

I sigh. I can't help it. This must be the night for uncomfortable conversations. "No. I already told you that."

"Do you want him to be?"

I don't know how to answer this. He asked me to be honest, and I want to be truthful without telling him the actual truth. "I wanted him to be, yes."

"Do you still?"

"Simon . . ." What I want or don't want doesn't really matter.

"No, I'm sorry. You don't have to answer that."

A part of me thinks this whole thing might be easier if I do answer, though, even if I don't tell him everything. "A lot of things changed between me and Ben after Trixie died. Sometimes it still hurts."

There's a pause, and then he says, "Oh, okay."

What I said must be enough for him.

Mosquitos buzz near my face and I swat at them. "We've got citronella candles in the shed. Bring those down next time." I reach over and smash one on his calf. "Don't you have mosquitos in St. Paul?"

I smile at him. He reaches across the arm of his chair and clasps my hand. This time, his hand is sweaty. This time, Ben's not around to see. This time, he means it.

I tug my hand away a minute later to slap at a mosquito on my neck. "I'm getting eaten alive here."

Simon stands up and smiles down at me. "I'll walk you home."

We walk up the hill toward my house and stop at the bottom of the stairs to the deck.

"There are so many stars here," he says. "It's so beautiful. I wish I could paint this."

He leans over and his lips touch my cheek in the slightest whisper of a kiss.

"Good night, Lucy."

Simon turns and walks across the grass. I watch until he ducks around the lilac bush, out of sight, my hand on my cheek.

I like him. I like his shaggy hair and his paint-stained fingers. He's nice to me and he wants to spend time with me.

I want to spend time with him.

That's got to count for something.

18 · Ben

GUTHRIE AND I STARTED HANGING OUT AT THE FULL LOON ON Monday nights a couple of months after Trixie died. I was so sick of being at home, of sitting across from my parents at dinner, struggling to find something to say that wouldn't remind them of Trixie, that I called up Guthrie and asked him to meet me there to watch *Monday Night Football*. And the next week and the week after that.

I don't even like football.

We ate there every Monday night, even after the football season ended.

Lucy doesn't usually work Monday nights. Last week had to be a fluke. I'm counting on it.

"Hey, Ben," Daniel says as I sit down at the counter. "How're the fish biting?"

"Good," I say. "Water levels are up after this week's rain."

"How are the folks?"

"Good," I say again, although this time it's not quite the truth. Mum had one of her days when she didn't get out of bed, and Dad flipped out at me when I scraped the Crestliner against the dock.

"You want the special?" Daniel asks, and I nod.

The special, Daniel's famous Onion Ring Barbecue Bacon Burger. Dad used to call it a heart attack on a plate, but we don't make jokes like that anymore.

We don't make any jokes anymore, come to think of it.

Guthrie slides onto the stool beside me. He's tall and lanky with dark copper hair and a broad forehead. He's part Irish, part Ojibwe, with a low, even voice. It takes a lot to get Guthrie riled.

"Hey," he says. "I'll have the same."

"What's up?" I ask.

"Well," he says, "me and Eddie drove up to Whitefish today. Caught a nice mess of walleye."

"Where at?"

He thinks for a minute. "Second weedline. About twelve feet. Fifteen maybe."

"Huh." Warmer temps and the walleye go deeper. He rattles on, this in-depth analysis of the air temperature in relation to the water temperature, the delay in weed growth this year.

"Eddie landed this giant crappie," he says. "You shoulda seen it. Biggest damn crappie I've ever seen."

"He keep it?"

"Nah, threw it back for somebody else to catch. You go out today?"

"Yeah. Took out a family with a couple of high school kids. The guy was a dick but the girl was okay." I pause. "Kinda cute."

Actually, she reminded me a little of Lucy, except her teeth were straight and she couldn't even bait her own hook. Not that I should be looking.

Not that I should be thinking about Lucy.

"So," he says, "did you end it with Dana?"

Whoa. What?

"End it with Dana? Where did you hear that?" My throat goes dry and I reach for my water glass.

"Oh, it's around, man. Rumor is that you've been hanging out with Lucy. Something about you two out on the lake together."

I nearly spit water all over the counter. "What?"

"Yeah. I've tried to dispel that rumor."

"So you don't believe it?"

God, what a stupid thing to say.

Guthrie gives me a dry look. "Why would I believe it?"

I don't answer. I shake my head.

"Am I missing something?" Guthrie asks. "You're checking out some girl at the resort. You're acting all weird about Lucy. What's going on?"

I shake my head again. "Nothing. I don't know what I'm saying. It doesn't mean anything."

"So did you and Dana break up?"

"No. But I did take Lucy out fishing. Lucy and *Emily*. It's my job."

Daniel sets two plates in front of us. I'm so hungry, the smell of bacon nearly turns my stomach inside out. For a minute all I can think about is how fucking awesome this burger is going to taste, but then something hits me.

"Wait. Is *Dana* telling people we broke up?"

Guthrie stuffs a handful of french fries into his mouth. He chews for a minute, swallows, and doesn't answer right away, as if he's giving serious consideration to my question.

"Are you in love with Dana?" he asks.

"Seriously, Guthrie? I think you know the answer to that question."

"I don't know that I do," he says.

He's trying to make me say it. I'm not going to say it. Hell, no, I'm not in love with Dana.

Dana's a sweet girl. There's no reason why I shouldn't love her. But I don't.

Guthrie takes a gigantic bite of his burger. I don't expect him to say anything right away anyway.

He's the youngest of five—he's got an older brother and three older sisters. Those girls—and their mom—talk a blue streak. And Guthrie—just like his dad and Eddie—learned early on to choose his words carefully.

When he's not fishing, he's reading. He never knew his Ojibwe grandfather, and in fourth grade, he decided to learn everything he could about his ancestors. He didn't stop there. He learned about other Native cultures and then moved on to German and Scandinavian immigrants, and French-Canadian trappers. He's like a walking Minnesota history book.

We both plow through the food on our plates and then Guthrie says, "Well, this, too, shall pass."

"You sound like my gram," I grumble.

Guthrie throws money on the counter and gets up. "Gotta go. I still have to gut those walleye."

I finish my burger and then a piece of pie that Daniel sets down in front of me without me asking for it—lemon meringue. I'm a simple guy, I guess, when it comes to pie. I like the classics, cherry and apple and lemon meringue.

Fuck if I know what that means.

I get in the Firebird.

I should drive over to Dana's and convince her that the rumor about me and Lucy isn't true. It wouldn't take much. Her parents are never home, not that it would matter if they were.

Maybe I *should* break up with her.

I stare at the empty passenger seat, and suddenly I'm thinking about Lucy again.

For the first time ever, I don't want to be in this car.

I drive over to Dana's, but I don't have the energy to break up with her. Not tonight.

19 · *Lucy*

HANNAH'S BACK FROM THE BOOK TOUR, SO WE SPEND Thursday night at her house, watching movies and catching up.

"I was hoping for a lot of hot cowboy action in Texas," she says, "but I was sadly disappointed. It was just one bookstore and hotel after another. My first and last book tour, promise. Let's watch *Young Guns*. I mean, those guys are hot, right?"

I shrug. I don't really care what movie we watch. I'm just happy she's back.

Trixie may have been a splendid torch, but Hannah's a wildfire.

"So, what's up with you and your mom? She was really giving you the cold shoulder," Hannah says. We'd stopped by the Full Loon to pick up the butterscotch pie she'd been craving since Texas. Mom didn't say one word to me; she hasn't spoken to me much since our conversation in the car.

I fill Hannah in.

"So she's pissed at you because you won't pick up that shift?" she asks.

"Yeah. I looked at the schedule and tried to juggle things around. I thought I'd come up with a decent solution, but that just pissed her off more."

"Has she always been like this?" Hannah asks. "At the restaurant 24/7?"

"No. She worked part time until my grandparents retired and she took over. Daniel was working at a brewpub in Minneapolis, and she convinced him to move back and help her. But then Clayton left for school, and then there were tuition bills to pay. She let her assistant manager go and basically lives there."

"So are you going to take that Monday night shift?"

I shake my head. "Nope. Standing my ground on this one, even if Mom doesn't talk to me for the rest of the summer."

"Good for you."

"Or maybe I'll quit."

Hannah laughs. "You won't quit, Lucille. You're too loyal."

Loyalty. My biggest flaw, apparently.

"You'll get over it and so will she, whether you pick up Monday nights or not."

It doesn't feel like we're getting over it.

"So . . . what else is new?" she says. "You see much of Simon the Renter?"

At this, my cheeks go warm, pink.

"Ha! I knew it! Spill."

I tell her about our date to Cloud 9 and the night at the beach.

"You kissed him, didn't you? I mean, how could you not? Cute boy, romantic night at the beach . . ."

I nod and am surprised to find that my lips turn up in a small smile. "Well, not really. He kissed my cheek."

"Close enough! When are you going to see him again?"

"I've seen him. He's right next door, remember?"

"No, I mean *see* him again. Like a date."

I shrug.

"Lucille. What have you got to lose?"

When I don't reply, she says in a soft, gentle voice, "You can't lose what you don't have, Lucy."

She's right. I know she's right.

I would write that one in the Book of Quotes if I still had it.

Hannah claps her hands together once. "Oh! I just remembered! There's a party at Guthrie's tomorrow night and you're going! And you should invite Simon the Renter!"

"Um, okay." I don't know enough about Simon to know if he's the party type, especially with a bunch of people he doesn't know. "I'll ask him tomorrow."

"No, Lucille. I mean right now! Text him right now!"

I do: *Party tmrw nite. Wanna go?*

I'm almost nervous for his reply, but I only have to wait a few seconds: *Hell yes.*

Hannah snatches the phone from me. "What did I tell you? You got this, Lucille."

There's a piece of me that feels brave and proud. Simon said yes.

20 · Ben

Friday night a bunch of us head out to Guthrie's. His brother Eddie's having a party. Dana brings her friends Gretchen and Kiersten along. I soon realize this is a huge mistake, because all that Dana's friends are capable of doing is ripping on every single person at the party. And the more they drink, the cattier they get.

The more I drink, the more I want to get the hell away from them.

"Oh my God," Gretchen says. "What are *they* doing here?"

I look over to see four people moving toward us, and one of them is Lucy.

"I can't believe she has the nerve to show her face." Kiersten's words are sharp. "After that whole boat ride incident?"

Gretchen snorts. "Like she actually believed she could steal Ben away from you, Dana."

Christ, I wish the two of them would shut up.

"I'm standing right here," I say.

"Really, guys." Dana's had a couple of drinks, too, but isn't acting like a complete bitch. "That was all a huge misunderstanding, wasn't it, Ben?"

I squint to get a better look. Even in the darkness of dusk, there's no mistaking Hannah Mills, long legs up to there, cowboy boots, skimpy top. Her blond hair is big, like Texas big, and loose. She's got her hick boyfriend on her arm, Dustin something. And right behind her is Lucy with the guy who was holding her hand at the Full Loon. The guy who took her to Cloud 9.

"Who does she think she is, anyway?" Kiersten slurs. "Nobody invited her. She's not even *friends* with anyone here."

"She's friends with Guthrie," I say. "And the last time I checked, nobody needs an invitation. Nobody invited you."

"Excuse me," Gretchen says. "Why are you defending her?"

"I'm not," I say.

"Seriously, Gretch, don't believe everything you hear." Dana leans over and kisses my cheek. "Right, Ben?"

"Yeah, sure."

Lucy and her friends are closer now. As they pass by, the dickhead reaches for Lucy's hand and she takes it.

Later, after almost everyone has left, including Dana and her sloppy-drunk friends, I walk down toward the woods to take a piss, and Lucy's sitting alone on the beach, slapping at mosquitos, a beer balanced on the arm of the camp chair someone's dragged down there.

I didn't know Lucy and her friends were still here.

I'm going to talk to her.

I'll just walk up to her and tell her that I'm sorry. Easy. And she'll forgive me and we can be friends again.

I'm drunk enough, I can pull this off.

But then Hannah comes out of nowhere, grabs Lucy and drags her up, spins her around in the sand, and shouts, "Lucille! Let's go for a swim!"

Hannah's already stripping off her tank top, a bikini underneath it.

No, I want to say, Lucy doesn't like to swim. She doesn't like the weeds.

Lucy shakes her head.

And then Guthrie is there—*Guthrie?*—and Hannah grabs his hand and they're splashing into the lake, and Lucy's alone again.

I take a step toward her but my path is blocked.

By that guy.

I don't remember his name.

"Hey," he says. "You're Ben, right?"

"Do I know you?" I'm not in the mood to be polite.

"We haven't met, not officially, but I know who you are."

"What do you want?"

"So, um, I think it would be good if you stayed away from Luce, okay?" His voice shakes like he's nervous.

"What the fuck is that supposed to mean?"

"It means, she's got enough going on in her life without having to, um, be confused about you, too."

He thinks he can just waltz into town and talk to me like this? He doesn't know Lucy, not like I do.

Like I used to.

"Who do you think you are?" I spit.

"Lucy's boyfriend," he says, his voice quivering.

He's been here, what? Two weeks? And he's her *boyfriend*?

He turns away and walks down to the beach to where she

stands, arms crossed, watching her friends splash in the lake. He puts his hands on her shoulders, turns her to face him, and leans in to kiss her.

Lucy's boyfriend.

Is not me.

21 · Lucy

FRIDAY NIGHT, SIMON IS OUR DESIGNATED DRIVER, BUT I don't drink, either. I need to keep an eye on Hannah, a firefly in the darkening night, flitting from one group to another.

She's having such a good time. I wish I could let go like she does, let myself be so carefree and loose. She and Guthrie stand in the lake and splash water at each other. Guthrie seems lighter, happier, too, with Hannah around.

"Hey."

It's Simon, his brow furrowed. He puts his hands on my shoulders, turns me into him.

"What's wrong?" I ask.

He doesn't answer, but bends toward me without hesitation and kisses me.

It's sweet and smoky and sends a shiver down my spine. I reach my arms up around his neck and then he's closer, warm, soft. Sweet.

He pulls away after a moment. "Nothing's wrong. Everything's perfect."

I bury my face in his chest, close my eyes, and let myself believe it.

The next afternoon, Clayton is in the living room with Dad when I get home from the resort.

"What are you doing here?" I ask.

"Nice to see you, too, sis." He tips a bottle of beer to his lips and takes a long drink. "Tomorrow's Father's Day. I thought I'd go out fishing with the old man."

Dad grins and they clink their bottles together.

"You're letting him drink?" I say, my hands on my hips. Dad shrugs.

"It's one beer, Lucy, lighten up." Clayton scowls at me. He can get away with anything. "Do you have your period or something?"

So typical.

Dad shakes his head. "I sure haven't missed all this bickering."

"Grow up, Clayton," I say.

Clay gives me the finger. "You're not letting her come fishing with us tomorrow, are you, Dad?"

I stomp up the stairs to my room. Two more years. Two more years before I can run away like he did.

After dinner, I hear them arguing.

"I'm in a tight spot," Clay says. "I could really use some help."

I tiptoe to the top of the stairs to hear more clearly. I'm expecting Dad to shell out the cash, whatever Clayton needs.

"You're in a tight spot?" Dad says. "You drove all this way to tell me you're in a tight spot? You've got to be kidding me. Your mom and I are working around the clock, Clay, to pay for your education. And then I hear that you get an incomplete? Lucy's right. It's time for you to grow up."

My jaw nearly hits the floor.

"C'mon, Dad, give me a break here."

"No. There isn't any money to give you, Clayton, although that's beside the point. If you need money so badly, maybe it's time for you to get a job."

"Oh, terrific," Clay says. "I come home for this? For nothing?"

I hear a door slam, and I go back to my room. I don't get the door closed in time before Clayton walks by.

"Unbelievable," he says.

I turn to face him. "No, you're unbelievable. You came home to see Dad on Father's Day, right? No? Nice, Clay. Real nice."

"Shut it," he growls at me. He goes into his room and is back seconds later, his backpack over his shoulder. "I'm outta here."

I'm not surprised at how Clay acted, but Dad's words stunned me. He's always given in to Clay, always let things slide with him because he was older, he was the boy, his buddy. And I've felt like I needed to be extra good to make up for Clayton. It's not fair, but that's the way it is. I'm amazed that Dad finally stood up to him, told him no.

A few minutes later Dad comes up and knocks on my door.

"Hey," he says. "So you heard all that, then, that business with your brother?"

I nod.

"He take off?"

I nod again.

"What do you say you and me go out and catch a few fish tomorrow? I've already got Daniel's boat."

I smile. "I'd like that." I think about Simon, how he's never been fishing, that his dad always promised to take him but was always too busy at the store. "Do you mind if Simon comes with? He's never fished before. And his dad—well, his parents have been divorced for a while."

Dad nods. "Sure, kiddo. That'll be fun."

When I pick up my phone to text Simon, there's a message from him: *Miss u.*

I decide to ask him to go fishing with us in person. I find my flip-flops by the front door and cross the driveway to Simon's house.

Sunday morning, Simon comes over after breakfast, bouncing on his heels in excitement. Dad hands him one of Clayton's old rods, and we head down the hill to the dock and Daniel's Alumacraft.

I flip up a seat cushion. "Here's your PFD," I tell him, handing him a camouflage vest.

"My what?"

"Personal flotation device." I slip on Clare's yellow one and demonstrate how to snap it shut and tighten the straps.

"Oh, a life jacket. It's been a long time since I've been out on a boat. Years, actually." He laughs, an uncomfortable, awkward sound. "I guess this isn't my thing, really."

He's not kidding. After we drop anchor, he struggles with the tackle and the reel and panics every time he gets a bite. But my dad is patient with him, like he was when he taught us, and eventually Simon fumbles through the process himself.

"So how's Halcyon Lake treating you and your mom, Simon?" Dad asks.

Simon bites his lower lip as he hooks a night crawler and casts out. "So far, so good."

I'm nervous for him—anxious that he won't catch anything and be disappointed in himself, worried that he and my dad won't have anything in common.

"You get to many Twins games?" It was only a matter of time before my dad brought up baseball.

"Never been. Not much of a sports fan, I guess."

Dad clears his throat. "Huh." There's a tug on Dad's line, though, so he turns his attention to the fish, which turns out to be a nice-size rock bass.

"Uh, are that thing's eyes red?" Simon leans closer to the fish with muddled bronze scales. Its harsh red eye against the whitish mouth is like something out of a horror movie.

"Yep. Pretty little thing, isn't it?"

I laugh at the look of disgust that crosses Simon's face.

Dad leans over the side of the boat to drop the fish back into the lake.

"You're not keeping it?"

"Nah, we'll let someone else have a little fun with him." Dad casts out again. "So, what do you do if you're not into sports?"

"Painting. I used to take piano lessons." His bobber sinks a little and he leans over, excited, but then, nothing. "Shoot. I watch a lot of movies. I'm kind of a James Bond aficionado."

"You like double-oh-seven?" There's excitement in Dad's

voice, and I know exactly what he'll say next. "Who's your favorite Bond?"

I hope that Simon gets this right.

"Well, I have to say that I'm really impressed with Daniel Craig, and you can't go wrong with the classic Sean Connery, but honestly? My favorite has always been Roger Moore."

Dad turns to Simon and grins. "That's what I like to hear."

There's a tug on Simon's line so hard, he's pulled forward and nearly loses his balance. I set down my rod and move to help him.

"Easy." I put my hand over his on the reel, and when we land a northern pike into the net, a smile spreads across his face so wide, I can't help but match it.

22 · Ben

FATHER'S DAY.

Another first without Trixie. Mother's Day sucked, and I don't expect today to be any better.

I wake up early. It's my day off, and even though Mum narrowed her eyes and pinched her lips when I told her yesterday, Guthrie and I are planning on taking out the pontoon and hitting up Story Lake for walleye.

Dad's downstairs, and, by the looks of it, he hasn't slept. He sits on the couch, his hand tight around an empty lowball tumbler. I walk past him, not saying anything, hoping that he won't notice.

But he does.

"Ben, son, c'mere." He's crying.

This is the worst I've seen him. He's drunk and he's crying and I can't handle this. It's fucking Father's Day, and I want to get the hell out of here. I don't want to see this; I don't want to acknowledge him, acknowledge what's happening to him.

I guess I'm not any better.

"What do you need, Dad?" My voice shakes. "You should get some sleep."

"Nah," he says, "I'm taking out that family today. The three generations?"

Uhhh. My stomach drops. He's supposed to work today. He insisted on it, even though John told him it wasn't necessary,

THE LAST THING YOU SAID

even offered me up for the job instead. But no, Dad wanted to take out the three generations of fishermen. I overheard him tell John that it would be good for him, would help him take his mind off things.

Things.

Things like today is his first Father's Day without his daughter. Goddamn it.

"Dad, what time are you supposed to go out?"

He thinks for a long time, lifts his empty glass to his lips and then sets it down again, disappointed. "Nine o'clock."

Less than an hour. Guess I'll be working after all.

"Come on." I help him up and walk him down the hall to the guest room. He'd never make it up the stairs, and I wouldn't want to wake up Mum anyway. I don't want to think about how she's going to react when she finds him on the spare bed, and I sure as hell don't want to be around for it.

"Thought Tom was taking us out," an old guy says when I meet the fishermen down at the dock and introduce myself. He's a grumpy old codger, his face reddened and weathered.

"That's my dad, sir," I tell him. "He's not feeling well, so I'm filling in for him."

"That right? I sure hope you know what the fuck you're doing, kid. We're paying a lot of money for this."

I can't help it. I laugh. "I sure as fuck do, sir. I grew up on this lake."

The middle one, the old codger's son, pats me on the back. "I think we're going to get along just fine."

The youngest is twenty-five, married with a baby, a boy. "Couple more years and he'll be out here with us. Four generations."

"I'll probably be dead by then," the old codger says.

His son shakes his head. "We should be so lucky."

I listen to their banter the rest of the morning. They know what they're doing, so basically my job is to move from hot spot to hot spot. Between the three of them, the well fills with fish quickly: perch, bluegills, even a couple of walleye.

We're about to pull anchor and head back to shore when the old man asks me, "So what's your story, kid?"

"Sir?" I'm not sure exactly which story he'd like to hear. The one about my drunk father? Or how about the time my sister died in this lake and I didn't get to her in time to save her? That's a good one.

"I mean, why the hell is a good-looking kid like you out here fishing with the three of us? You got nothing better to do?"

Sounds about right.

I don't know why, but I tell him the truth. "It's my home, this lake. It's the only place I want to be these days. The only place where I don't need to give a shit about anything."

He narrows his eyes at me and nods. "And you better be damn grateful for it."

"I am, sir." I pull up anchor.

The Promise

One warm summer day, Trixie and Lulu, who were older now, packed a picnic lunch and walked to their favorite park, with rolling green hills, endless trees, and their beloved lake. They ran through the park, long hair and a dusting of silver and gold trailing behind them. They turned cartwheels. They twirled, arms wide, their faces to the sky. They searched for four-leaf clovers and found dozens, which they set in a pile on their plaid picnic blanket. They sat close together and were warmed by the patch of sun that streamed through the trees.

"Lulu," Trixie said, "I want to talk to you about Ben."

Lulu looked up in surprise. "What about him?" she asked, anxious. They didn't often talk about Ben or Lulu's feelings for him.

"I know it must be hard for you, seeing him with other girls."

Lulu didn't say anything.

"He'll come around," Trixie said. "I know my brother, Lulu. Be patient."

Lulu pulled her knees up to her chest and rested her chin on them. "How can you be so sure, Trix? Sometimes he talks to me, sometimes I wonder if he notices I'm even there."

"Trust me, he notices. And someday, he will love you as much as you love him. As much as I love you. I promise."

For a long time, Lulu didn't say anything. She picked at the fringe at the edge of the blanket. She thought about what

Trixie had said—that she should be patient, that Ben would figure it out. But what if he didn't? What if Lulu waited, but Ben never learned to love her? What then?

Trixie scooped up the pile of clovers. "Hold out your hands, Lulu."

Lulu did, and Trixie dropped the clovers. They poured down and multiplied and spilled out over the edges of Lulu's fingers.

"For luck," *Trixie said.* "I promise you."

"Trixie, how can you be so sure it's going to happen?"

"I know it. I know it in my heart."

JULY

What we have once enjoyed we can never lose.
All that we love deeply becomes a part of us.
—*Helen Keller*

23 · Ben

GUTHRIE'S BROTHER EDDIE THROWS A PARTY EVERY FOURTH of July. He and his buddies set off fireworks from an island in the middle of Story Lake that will forever be known as Firecracker Island. The morning of the Fourth, we're roasting hot dogs over the campfire for breakfast, and I ask Eddie if I can shoot them off, too.

He laughs. "There's not much to it. They're wired together, so we only light it once. It's mostly work up front. Manual labor. You up for that?"

"Yeah."

Eddie's head is cocked to one side, and he's got this look on his face like something is off. "You know it's illegal, right?"

I shrug. "So?"

"You could get in a shitload of trouble if we get caught."

"Dude," I say. "You've been doing this for what, three years? You really think some cop is going to drive his ass all the way out here to bust you?"

"Uh, ever hear of water patrol?"

"I know all of 'em," I say. "They're too lazy to bother coming out this far."

"Well, whatever. It's your funeral."

There's a pause.

"You know what I mean," he says, his face bright red.

• • •

Late afternoon, Guthrie and me, Eddie, and some of his hockey buddies load the fireworks and equipment onto the pontoon and a beat-up old speedboat. We make three trips out to the island.

Eddie wasn't kidding about manual labor. It's hot, and before we've unloaded the first haul, I've got sweat running down my back. I strip off my shirt and carry another of Eddie's custom-made wooden crates over to the clearing on the beach. Each group of fireworks is on a separate plywood plank or wooden crate, labeled one to twenty-six.

"There's no thirteen," I tell Guthrie. He's carrying number four, a dozen Roman candles.

"Eddie's superstitious," he says. "I don't blame him. Bad luck and pyrotechnics don't mix."

"Drinking and pyrotechnics don't mix, either, but I see that hasn't stopped them."

"Eddie's not drinking today. Me neither."

"When do you?" I ask. "I'll drink enough for the both of us."

"Where's Dana today?"

I lean over into the boat for number seven, layer cakes. "Apparently I'm not as irresistible as she originally thought. She's shopping with her mom and her sisters at the Mall of America."

"That sounds miserable." He picks up a box and laughs. "Check this out. God of Fire. Warning: shoots flaming balls. This is gonna be so good."

• • •

By the time everything's wired and ready to go, Guthrie's back-yard and beach are crawling with people.

"You might as well watch from down there," Eddie tells me and Guthrie and points to the shore. "Like I said, we light it once and the rest takes care of itself."

"How much did you spend on this shit?" I ask.

Eddie shrugs. "About a grand, I think."

Shit. If I had an extra grand lying around, I sure as hell wouldn't use it to buy fireworks.

"All that money, all that time, and what do you get? Twenty-five, thirty minutes?"

"If that," Eddie says. "But it's a freaking amazing thirty minutes." He waves his arms over the platform of fireworks. "This setup is a work of art. It takes a lot of time and know-how to create the perfect sequence, you know?"

"Doesn't seem worth it."

"Is anything we do worth the effort we put into it?" Eddie says. "Say you sit out on the boat all day and never get a single bite. Worth it?"

"Never happens," I joke.

"I'm speaking in generalizations," Eddie says. "Sometimes it's about the experience, you know?"

The experience.

We move our camp chairs down to the shore. I'm not drunk. I thought maybe by now I would be. But I'm tired. I push up from the chair and stretch out on the cool sand.

There's nothing like summer in Minnesota lake country. The air is humid and still. The wake of a slow-moving pontoon laps against the shore in a gentle rhythm.

"Everybody set?" Eddie yells, and the first of the shells launches.

I think about what he said, about how sometimes it's more about the experience, even if the show only lasts for a fraction of the time it took to prepare for it.

The sky fills with blinking, flashing sparks of white.

"Nice," Guthrie says. "Diamonds."

A mosquito buzzes in my ear. I slap at it and another one on my arm.

"Lucy," I say. It comes out of nowhere. I haven't thought about her all day. "There's a song, right, something about Lucy and diamonds in the sky?"

Guthrie laughs. "Something like that."

24 · Lucy

SIMON GOES HOME FOR THE FOURTH OF JULY, SO I SPEND THE night at Hannah's. We sit on the deck, waiting for sundown and the fireworks over Halcyon Lake.

"So do you miss your boyfriend?" she asks, handing me a glass of lemonade.

"Yes." I take a tentative sip. "What's in this?"

"Vodka, what else?" She sits down. "Are you in love with him?"

I shrug. "I don't know."

"Well, I suppose we could try to figure that out. We've got all night." She picks up her phone from the arm of her deck chair and starts tapping on the screen. "Let's see, searching for *are you in love quiz*."

"Hannah . . ."

"Here we go. 'Number one: *When you first saw your special someone, you A. Thought he was cute. B. Didn't find him attractive but he grew on you. C. Didn't give him a second look. D. Were deeply attracted to him.*'"

I roll my eyes and Hannah laughs.

"'Number two: *How often do you think of your sweetheart when you're apart?*' 'Sweetheart'? What is this, the 1940s? '*A. Every waking moment. B. Several times a day. C. Once or twice a day. D. Hardly ever.*' Well, Lucille? Your answer?"

"Hannah."

"Fine." She continues to scroll. "Oh, wait, one more. This one's perfect for you. '*Your sweetheart gives you a romantic card. What do you do with it? A. Sleep with it under your pillow. B. Scrapbook it. C. File it away. D. Toss it.*'"

I slip my hand into my pocket and find the agate. I haven't told Hannah about it. "Would you stop already?"

"Don't you want to know?"

"I'm not going to find out from some quiz you found on the Internet." I pause. None of these questions sound like anything I would ask myself about Simon—well, maybe the one about thinking he was cute. He is definitely cute. But . . .

Deeply attracted.

Every waking moment.

Carry it in my pocket.

I take a long drink of my lemonade. It's strong, and the alcohol swirls through me, loosens me. "What about you? Is Dustin your *special someone?*"

She laughs. "I don't need to take a quiz to know I'm not in love with Dustin. He's fun and we always have a good time, but Dustin is not true-love material, at least not for me. And shoot, who says it has to be true love, anyway? I just want to have a good time, try new things, meet new people. Nothing wrong with that, am I right?"

"I guess not."

"You like Simon, though, right? You have fun with him?"

I do. He's sweet and attentive. He takes me to the movies, we play mini-golf even though he has not improved, I sit at the lakeside patio with him while he paints. It's one of the things I like best about him, how he's able to capture his surroundings in watercolor and acrylic. Sometimes we walk down to the beach between our houses, sheltered from view by thick trees, and kiss, falling to the sand, until our lips are bruised and our breaths come heavy.

"Yes. I like him."

Her glass is empty, so she reaches for mine and takes a drink. "Lucille, it's okay to like Simon. If not Simon, some other guy. You don't need anyone's permission."

What she doesn't say: especially Ben's permission. She's right.

"And nobody said it had to be love," she continues.

I blow out a long breath. The idea of falling in love with Simon—of falling in love with anyone but Ben—scares me. The swirl spirals down, reaches my toes, but now it's more than looseness, it's relief, too. Nobody said it had to be love.

But there's plenty of summer left for me and Simon, and I'm going to make the best of it. "I know."

"Just remember that, okay?" She shakes her big blond hair. "Want to watch the fireworks from the middle of the lake? Dad got us a new paddleboat."

A few days after the Fourth, I'm eating breakfast at the resort and Tami announces, "Our nephew is getting married in Duluth in a couple of weeks, and I wondered if you would like to come along to help with Emily."

"Sure," I say, not at all sure. The first question that comes to mind is—which side of the family, John's or Tami's? If it's

John's nephew, the cousin I met on vacation last year, then Ben and his parents will be there.

"We'll go up Friday morning and come home Sunday." She prattles on about the hotel and the church and the rehearsal but never once says who's getting married. After a few minutes, I put up my hand to stop her.

"Whose wedding?" I ask.

"Aaron. You've met him, haven't you?"

Ben's cousin. I nod.

Tami is talking nonstop. "This will be a nice little getaway for you, and you won't have to take care of Emily the whole time. You'll have some free time, too. Our hotel is right on the harbor. We're getting two rooms so you and Emily would have a room to yourselves. A suite, actually, so after she goes to sleep you can stay up and watch a movie or something."

I nod. I'm their nanny. Of course they expect I'll go away for the weekend with them. And I love Duluth, I love Lake Superior.

"I'm so glad you'll come with us. This is just what you need, a little time away. And maybe—maybe if you and Ben get some time together—"

"What?" The air is suddenly stifling. What is she saying? Did she invite me along to try to patch things up between Ben and me?

Tami has this terrible, pitying look on her face. "Oh, Lucy, I know how hard it's been since Trixie died. My heart breaks for you. You lost your best friend. And Ben—well, I don't know what happened between you two, but I know that you aren't friends anymore. And maybe—maybe if you had a chance to talk about it away from here—"

"No," I say. "Please, stop."

"Lucy—"

I can't talk to her about this anymore. "Emily's waiting for me in the tree house. I have to go." I open the sliding door and step out onto the deck, down the stairs, across the yard to the old oak tree.

I climb up and sit on the worn floorboards of the tree house, my back against the plywood wall, while Emily plays tea party, and I catch my breath. I think about the trip to Duluth with Trixie's family last summer, one of the best weekends of my life.

At the cabin, Trixie and I skipped stones on the lake while Ben sifted through the rocky beach.

"Agates are quartz, you know," Ben said. "And they're pretty unique here because of the iron in the soil. The oxidation of the iron gives them that reddish-orange color. You want to help me look?"

I glanced at Trixie. She was smiling. "Sure," I said.

"Did you know that the Lake Superior agate is Minnesota's state gemstone?" Ben asked. "The agates were formed about a billion years ago. From lava eruptions. No, really, a billion years ago."

I nodded and smiled as he told me about glacial movement and why Lake Superior agates can be found in other regions of the state, thrilled that he was talking to me about something he loved.

Later that weekend, we stopped at a lapidary shop in Beaver Bay filled with bin after bin of agates and other rocks. Ben must have spent an hour poring over each and every one, examining, humming to himself. After a while, Trixie and I got tired of waiting for him and left to buy ice cream cones from the diner next door.

We sat on the bench outside the agate shop, licking the dripping ice cream from the sides of our waffle cones.

"Rocks are boring," Trixie said.

"I don't know," I said. "The agates are pretty."

"You're only saying that because you like Ben," she whispered, and gave me a knowing smile over her ice cream.

When Ben finally came out of the shop, he asked, "Where's mine?" Then he pointed at me. "Maple nut, right?"

I popped the last bit of waffle cone in my mouth and nodded.

"Finally!" Trixie said. "What took so long?"

Ben smiled. "I couldn't leave until I found what I was looking for."

Trixie rolled her eyes.

He looked at me and pointed to the corner of his mouth. "You've got ice cream on your face, Lu." He turned to walk to the van.

My face burned, and I scrubbed at my mouth with a napkin.

"Come on." Trixie pulled on my arm. "Let's get out of here."

Ben slid the door of the van open. Trixie climbed in and I started to follow her.

"Wait," Ben said. He tugged me back behind the van and pressed something into my hand.

I looked at the object in my palm. It was the most beautiful thing—an odd-shaped agate, not quite an oval, not even an inch wide. The stone was polished to a bright shine, a deep rusty red with bands of ivory and pink and gray that together formed an L.

"Oh," I gulped. "Is this for me?"

What a stupid thing to say.

"Well, yeah." Ben smiled.

"It's perfect," I said, and I meant it. Everything about the agate was perfect—the irregular shape, the coloring, the fact that Ben had chosen it just for me. My heart pounded. "Thank you."

Thank you. That's all I could say. I should have said more, but not there, not in front of Trixie and his parents.

Something was happening between us.

"Are you getting in or what?" Trixie called from inside the van and I turned, slipping the most perfect thing in the world into my pocket.

I didn't want Trixie to see. I didn't want her to know. This was special, between Ben and me. It was the only secret I had from her, ever.

For a long time, as we drove along the shore of Lake Superior, I didn't speak. I couldn't. I gazed out over the vast blue water and thought about Ben, who sat beside me, silent. I was in agony, not knowing what he was thinking. Wanting to say more, to ask him if he happened to see this agate and thought of me, or if he set out to find me the perfect agate and this, the one with the L, was it? A tiny miracle in a bin of small, polished stones.

I never asked.

I wonder how many hundreds of agates Ben has collected. I wonder if he thinks about my agate, the agate with the L. L for Lulu, L for love. I wonder if he thinks about me, what we almost had.

I wonder what he was about to say to me the day that Trixie died, just as Clayton yelled for us that he couldn't find her.

I'll never know.

Now, in the tree house with Emily, I take the agate out of the pocket of my jeans. I roll it over and over between my index finger and thumb.

25 · Ben

Tami catches me as I'm getting into the car to go home after a long day out on the lake. I was with a couple of guys who complained the whole time about how subpar the experience was compared to some isolated, fly-in-only lodge up in Saskatchewan. I'm hot, I stink, and I'm crabby.

"Ben, wait a minute," she says. She's barefoot and drying her hands on a dish towel. "Can you tell your mom that we need to pick up Lucy on Friday, so we'll just plan on meeting them at the rehearsal dinner?"

Why do they need to pick up Lucy? What does she have to do with the wedding?

"Lucy?"

"Oh, I didn't tell you? She's coming along to help with Emily."

Lucy's going to the wedding. Shit.

"Oh. Yeah, I'll tell Mum."

"Thanks, Ben. I've got to get back inside before the spaghetti boils over. See you tomorrow."

I get in the hot car and slam the door.

I haven't been back to Duluth since that last trip before Trixie died. Trixie begged to have Lucy come along, and I'm glad she did. I was sixteen and girl crazy, although last summer, it was more than girl crazy. Right before that trip, it hit me. I knew Lulu liked me. I'd known for a long time, since before she'd started leaving fudge on my desk. I knew then that I liked her, too. It was so natural, so *right*.

What I loved about Lulu: her laugh, her smile. Her white teeth, perfectly straight except for those two on the bottom, which bothered her even though no one noticed unless she pointed it out. Her long brown hair. I loved how she got irritated with herself whenever she forgot to put it up before we went out on the boat, and how she would braid it and tie the end with fishing line. I loved how she could spend an entire day out on the boat and never get bored, how her freckles popped out across her nose after all those hours in the sun. I loved that look she got in her eyes when she was excited or interested or amazed. She could lock eyes with you, and you'd feel like you never wanted her to look away.

I loved when she looked at me like that.

Like that day on the shore of Lake Superior when we found the inuksuit, at least fifty of them, on the rocky beach. She watched me with wide eyes as I tried to make my own stack, tried to balance the porous rocks, and then she tried, too, laughing as they collapsed and knocked mine over.

"I'm sorry, I'm sorry." And she laughed, high and light, and it was the most beautiful sound.

I never wanted to move from that spot, next to Lulu on the shore.

I loved her.

In Duluth, everything was good. Trixie was alive, and we didn't know what summer would bring. Lulu was with us, happy and amazed by the expanse and energy of Lake Superior.

This trip to Duluth will be different. Trixie's gone. Lucy isn't Lulu anymore, and I've got no one to blame but myself.

I start the Firebird and drive home to give Mum the message from Tami.

26 · Lucy

BEN'S COUSIN AARON GETS MARRIED IN A MASSIVE CATHEDRAL that overlooks Lake Superior. It's a cloudy, windy day, but Aaron and his bride María don't seem to mind. They are a vision of love and happily ever after. I stand outside and watch while the photographer takes picture after picture in the cold and wind.

When John and Tami are ready to go to their seats, by unluck of the draw, Ben is the usher up next to walk me down the aisle. He holds out his arm, and my hand shakes as I place it near his elbow. Beneath the fabric of his suit coat, his muscles tense; my hand instantly warms, a welcome sensation after the cold wind on the front steps of the church. We follow Tami on the arm of another usher, John with Emily. When we get near the front, I let go of Ben's arm and am cold once again. I look up at him. I wonder if he felt it, too, but there is no emotion in his eyes.

Jane and Tom sit in the pew in front of us. Jane turns around as the wedding march begins and for the briefest moment catches my eye. Hers are filled with tears, but she smiles. As the ceremony begins, she slips her arm through Tom's and rests her head on his shoulder.

Of course. This must be agonizing for them.

Tom will never walk his daughter down the aisle. Jane will never be the mother of the bride.

The ceremony is long, traditional, beautiful. John stands in an imposing marble pulpit to read a passage from the Bible, and I feel out of place, out of sorts. Emily squeezes my hand as her father reads, his words booming through the microphone and echoing to the far back corners of the church. She claps when he's done, then looks around, embarrassed, when no one joins in her applause. I stroke her hair and kiss the top of her head, filled with so much love for this little girl who reminds me of Trixie.

As I'm walking into the reception with Emily, Jane catches me.

"Oh, Lucy, sweetheart, it's so nice to see you." She pulls me into a hug. I stand, stiff, not sure what to do. When she steps back, I'm relieved. "You look absolutely lovely. How are you, my dear?"

"I'm—I'm okay," I whisper.

She tilts her head, considering me, what she'll say next. "I'm sorry, I have to go. Tom and I are the host and hostess, you see, but I'll come find you later. I'd love to hear—" She falters, then says, "Well, I really must go."

She's so wonderful, Trixie's mom, and I'm a terrible person. I haven't gone to see her. I've been so wrapped up in my own grief, I haven't considered hers or Tom's.

Emily takes my hand. "C'mon, Luce, let's go find Mom and Dad."

Later, after the dinner and toasts to the couple's happiness, after the first dance and more photographs, Emily pulls me out on the dance floor with Tami.

"She's doing great," I say to Tami. We'd been worried she would get tired and cranky after a long day at the church. I was certain we'd be back in our hotel room by now.

"It's because you're here," Tami says.

Emily grabs our hands and we swing together. She sees Ben and drags him over. He joins our circle in between Tami and Emily, directly across from me, but he doesn't look at me. The music changes to a slow song and Ben scoops Emily into his arms. They sway together and Emily squeals. Tami smiles and takes my hand as we walk back to the table.

"Thank you so much for coming with us," she says as we sit down. "It wouldn't be the same without you. You're part of the family." Her voice sounds a little sad at the last part, and I know she's thinking of Trixie.

I nod, too choked up by her words to speak. I take a drink from my water glass. The ice has melted; I watch flakes of minerals swirl in the water.

My phone buzzes. Simon has been sending text messages all day. Friday morning, before John and Tami picked me up, he kissed me hard and said, "I'm going to miss you, Lucy. I'll think about you while I feed my sorrow with pie at the Full Loon."

"I'll only be gone two days, Simon," I'd said.

"Two and a half. And you'll be with Ben all weekend." His words were lined with jealousy.

I furrowed my brows. "There's nothing to worry about."

"I hope not," he said with a lift of one eyebrow.

Hope you're having a good time, Simon's text reads. *Call me later.*

I'm about to reply when I look up, and Ben's standing at my chair, his hand held out. I suck in a breath.

Emily hops on one foot next to him. "Ben wants to dance with you, Lucy." She bounces to the other foot.

For a moment, I am unable to move. I don't know if I can be that close to him.

I need to be close to him.

I tremble as he leads me out to the dance floor. The music is slow and romantic and he takes me in his arms and it's like a dream. He places his hands on either side of my waist, and I slip my arms up around his neck, Simon's messages and kisses forgotten.

In this moment, it's almost as if last summer hasn't changed us. I close my eyes and imagine what this day would have been like if Trixie hadn't died. Maybe Ben wouldn't have pushed me away. Maybe we would have been together since that afternoon on the float, when he'd tugged on my ponytail and started to say something, something important, I'm sure of it. Maybe I would have been invited to this wedding not as Emily's nanny but as Ben's girlfriend. I would have been included in the family photograph, Ben's arm around my waist, instead of standing off to the side, out of the shot.

His fingers move, tighten against the fabric of my dress, press into me, and a strong current moves up my back. I shiver and wish that he could hold me like this forever.

The song ends, too soon, and Ben says nothing. He offers me his arm and we walk back to the table.

Our moment is over, but I can still feel his hands on me—on

my waist, my arm, everywhere he touched me and didn't. We haven't said a word to each other.

Emily still hops. "Ben, will you dance with me again?"

"Emily," I say, "do you need to powder your nose?"

She nods.

"I'll take her," Tami says.

I shake my head. "I'll go." I need a minute, a chance to catch my breath and come back to reality. I reach for my small beaded purse, but my hand shakes and it falls. Everything inside spills onto the floor—my lip gloss, a few coins, a tin of mints, the agate.

Oh no.

The agate.

I kneel down quickly to retrieve it, but Ben does, too, and we bump heads.

"I'm so sorry." I reach for the agate, but he gets to it first.

He picks it up, holds it in his palm. With the index finger of his other hand, he traces the L.

"Why is this in your purse?" he asks. His voice is tight.

"Because I don't have a pocket in this dress," I say, and I realize how ridiculous that sounds.

"I mean, why do you have it with you?" he says, softer.

"I always have it with me. Always," I whisper. I scoop the rest of my things into the purse and stand up, glad for a reason to get away from him. But Emily and Tami are already gone, walking hand-in-hand out of the reception hall.

"Oh," I say in a rush of breath. I feel dizzy from standing

too quickly, and Ben reaches out to steady me as I sway. His fingers on my arm send a jolt right to my empty, aching, broken heart.

Now Ben knows about the agate, that I still love him, even though I've tried not to. I need air. I need to be able to breathe again. I wrench my arm out of his grasp as I turn and run out past the lobby to the patio.

It's cool here behind the hotel, right on the lake. I head toward an empty bench but don't make it that far before I hear him.

"Lucy, wait," Ben calls.

I stop, there's nothing else I can do. He overtakes me and stands in front of me, his eyes locked on mine. He looks so handsome in his tux, the tie loose around his neck, his curls starting to rebel against whatever product has tamed them today.

"I—I need some air," I tell him, and I feel like such a fool.

I tuck my chin down so I don't have to look at him anymore, but he puts one finger lightly under my chin and pulls me up again. I'm afraid he'll try to kiss me. I'm afraid, and I want it more than anything.

"Okay."

He reaches for my hand, turns it palm up, and sets the agate in the center. He closes my fingers around it. I hold my breath, wait for him to say something.

Finally, he does. "So that guy, Simon? Is he your boyfriend, then?"

I hesitate before I answer. "Yes."

For a long moment, he doesn't say anything. Then his eyes narrow. "Does *he* know you carry that around with you?"

"What?"

"The agate. Does Simon know you carry the agate around with you?"

"N-no," I stammer.

"You should be careful, Lucy. You wouldn't want to give your boyfriend any reason to be jealous." His words are sharp, mocking.

When I don't speak, he keeps going. "Not that the agate means anything."

My stomach twists. His words echo what he said to me in the car that day. He took my already shattered heart and completely obliterated it.

The agate means everything.

I can't stand to be near him. Five minutes ago, I couldn't be close enough to him; I wanted him to hold on to me forever. And now—

"You *asshole*."

He flinches and he closes his eyes, but not before I see that he's hurt.

Good. I want him to be hurt.

He turns and walks back into the hotel, and I'm alone on the Lakewalk.

I can't breathe.

I should be careful? It's much too late for that. I should have been careful years ago, before Ben broke my heart.

• • •

When I go back into the reception hall, Emily has crashed. She's on Tami's lap, her head slumped against Tami's shoulder, her eyes slits. She wakes, and I take her by the hand to lead her to the elevators, grateful to make my escape.

This isn't how the night should have gone. Ben should have avoided me like he always does, given Emily any number of excuses not to dance with me.

I open my fist, close it again around Ben's agate.

Before the elevator reaches our floor, I've decided: I won't give Simon any reason to be jealous.

27 · Ben

SHE'S RIGHT, I'M AN ASSHOLE.

I walk away from her, my heart in my throat, my agate in her hand. God, she has the agate. She always has it with her.

Why do I keep finding ways to fuck this up?

As soon as I get back to the reception, I find Aaron.

"Hey," I say, "can you vouch for me at the bar?"

My cousin grins and nods as Nate, his best man, says, "I can do ya one better, little man. Come on out to the parking lot."

Aaron is intercepted by María on our way out, but the best man and I meet up with another groomsman who has a mini-bar set up on the tailgate of a black Silverado pickup.

"What's your poison?" Nate asks me, and I reach for a smallish bottle of tequila. No sense in fucking around.

"You sure about that?" Nate says.

I nod.

"Take that outta here," the other groomsman says. "And if anyone asks, you didn't get it from us."

I give him a salute and tuck the bottle in the inside pocket of my tux. I find a bench on the Lakewalk, close to where I'd left Lucy, but I figure she won't still be there and I'm right.

I sit there under the dim light of the streetlamp and listen to the waves of Lake Superior crash against the shore. Over and over. I imagine that the waves wash away the guilt and stupidity and grief, especially the grief. Washing it all away, numbing me. Or maybe it's the tequila, not the waves.

That bottle of tequila and I become good friends.

We have a really fun time together out on the Lakewalk, me and my friend tequila, and then a bridesmaid, María's little sister, joins us.

Little Sister: Hey, you.

Me: Hey.

Little Sister: Whatcha got there?

Me (holds up the bottle): This is my good friend, tequila.

Little Sister (grabs the bottle, downs the last few swallows): Nice to meet you, tequila. I'm Alicia.

Me: Ah-lee-see-ah.

Little Sister (dabbing at the corners of her mouth): Your friend is nice, but I'd rather get to know *you*, Ben.

She knows my name. She has a really wide, beautiful smile. Like the moon glistening on the water. Bright. Blinding.

"I like you," she says, and that's enough for me. We make out on the bench for a while and smoke cigarette after cigarette, but when she says she wants to go up to my room with me, I laugh, coughing on the smoke I just inhaled.

"I'm sure my parents would *love* that," I say.

"Your parents? How *old* are you?"

"Does it matter? How old are *you*?"

She scowls at me and adjusts her dress. She stands up and walks away, and I don't stop her. She left her pack of cigarettes and that makes us square, I guess, since she drank the last of my tequila.

The rest of the night is hazy, but somehow I make it back up to the hotel suite before my new best friend revolts. I spend a couple of hours on the cool bathroom floor but wake up in the bed, still in my tux with an ashtray mouth, a pounding headache, and a pool of acid in the pit of my stomach.

I deserve it, just like I deserve every bad name Lulu calls me.

I fall asleep or pass out, whichever, with her name on my numb lips.

What seems like only minutes later, Mum pulls me out of bed and tells me I need to hustle to get ready for the gift opening.

"Why do I have to go?" I mumble.

"You're in the wedding party, that's why. Now get going."

At breakfast, I can barely stomach the smell of waffles and eggs. I sit down next to Dad with a cup of coffee and a hard-boiled egg. He shakes his head and opens his mouth like he's going to say something, but I cut him off.

"Save it," I tell him. "I'm sure you'll have plenty of other opportunities to rag my ass this summer."

Lucy's here with John and Tami and Emily, but they're at a table across the room and Lucy has her back to me. Which is good.

And the bride's little sister, *Ah-lee-see-ah*, she's here, too, shooting daggers at me. She leans close to María and whispers in her ear. María looks in my direction and laughs.

My time with the bridesmaid—and the tequila, for that matter—is even hazier this morning.

But everything leading up to that point?

Crystal fucking clear.

Like when we posed for our family picture out on the steps of the church, and I had the craziest thoughts. Like: *Lucy should be in the photo. She belongs with us.*

Or even worse, when I walked her down the aisle before the ceremony began and I thought, *Someday we'll do this again.* Her fingers trembled against my arm, and I wanted to take her hand, hold it in between mine, and tell her that I'm sorry. I'm sorry, and I want to marry her.

Jesus.

And then, when I thought it couldn't get any worse, it did.

Lucy looked gorgeous and Emily wanted me to dance with her. And when could I ever say no to that girl? Either of them.

And before I knew it, I had the girl we used to call Lulu in my arms. She looked beautiful. She smelled like wildflowers. She fit into my arms like it was meant to be. I could have danced with her forever, and I hoped that the DJ would play another slow song so I could keep my girl close.

My girl. Lulu is not my girl.

I could hold her like that at a wedding, but not in our real lives. In real life, we are too damaged.

Mum is not happy with me, her mouth turned down in a constant frown. I should feel guilty—her daughter gone and her son a disappointment. I feel nothing but the lingering effects of the booze and too many cigarettes and the need to get the hell out of this place.

But why am I in such a hurry to get back home, where things are even worse?

28 · Lucy

LATE SUNDAY AFTERNOON, JOHN AND TAMI DROP ME OFF AT home. It's been a long day. At the fancy gift-opening breakfast, Ben looked like hell and didn't glance in my direction, not once. Emily was overtired and irritable on the drive home.

I'm thankful that my mom gave me the night off, even though she had to cover my shift herself. I'm looking forward to a hot shower, a quiet evening with a good book, and a full day off tomorrow.

I'm not surprised to find Simon sitting on the steps of my front porch, his long legs stretched out, earbuds in his ears. He hops up when he sees me, pulls out the earbuds, and grabs my suitcase.

"Let me carry that for you."

"How long have you been waiting here?"

"Not long." He smiles, a slow smile that lights up his whole face. "I missed you, Lucy." Inside, he sets the suitcase at the bottom of the stairs, then reaches his hand toward me and raises one eyebrow. He pulls me close and kisses me, slowly, gently. His kisses are sweet and comforting.

But I still feel Ben's arms around my waist as we danced, his touch, the arc of electricity straight to my battered heart. I shake the thought away.

When Simon pulls away from me, he asks in a whisper, "Are you—are you okay?"

"Yes." Not really.

He smiles. "How was the wedding?"

"Good, fine, okay."

"Wow, that good?"

Of course I can't tell him the truth. "Wonderful," I lie. "I love Duluth so much. And the wedding was beautiful."

"Want to come over to watch a movie tonight?"

"I'm really tired," I tell him. "Tomorrow night?"

He smiles. "Promise?"

He's satisfied with my nod and kisses me good-bye. "I'll take you out for pie," he says.

I carry my suitcase upstairs to my room and collapse onto my stomach on the bed, exhausted. The agate in my pocket digs into my thigh. I sit up and take it out. I place it in one palm and trace the L.

Oh, Ben.

I get up and walk over to my dresser. On the top is a small cedar treasure chest with an image of Split Rock Lighthouse on the lid, another souvenir from last year's trip to the North Shore. It's filled with small stones and agates that I collected on the beach. I set Ben's agate there among the ordinary rocks, take a deep breath, and close the lid.

I've just gotten out of the shower and into my pajamas when Hannah calls.

I give her the two-minute version of my weekend, and she says, "I'll be right over."

I want to be alone after a weekend of not having one

minute to myself, to fall into bed and sleep for days, but I need my Hannah, too. I wait for her in the living room.

She walks into the house without knocking, balancing two Dairy Queen Blizzards while she opens the door. She hands me one, then sits down in my dad's recliner.

"Spill," she says. "I want all the dirty details."

I tell her everything, even the part about the agate. Nothing would make sense if I left out the agate. I never even told Trixie about it.

"Wait," she says. "You've been carrying around an *agate*? A *rock*? Every day? For, like, a year?"

"Basically. Yes."

"In your pocket."

"Yes."

"For a boy you've never even kissed?"

I feel the heat rushing up from my neck.

"*Ohmygod Lucille,* you *kissed* Ben and never told me?" she yells, so loud I'm sure Simon can hear across the yard. "When?"

"It was nothing," I say.

"It was *not* nothing. Come on, tell me."

I swallow against the hot, teary feeling in my throat. "After her funeral. He gave me a ride home and he—he kissed me."

"Like, right after her funeral?"

"Yes."

"And then?"

And then.

And then he shattered me.

I shake my head.

"He hurt you," Hannah says. She doesn't push. "Oh, hon, you are so gone on that boy."

I sigh and set my cup on the end table next to the sofa. "Ben isn't going to happen. That's just the way it is. And besides, I have a boyfriend, remember? Simon?"

"Oh, sweetheart." She pauses, then says, "You know what you need? You need to get away from this place."

"I just got back."

She huffs. "Let me rephrase that. You need to get away from Ben. You need a rodeo."

"A rodeo?"

"Is there an echo in here? Damn right, a rodeo. Nothing cheers me up like seeing a hot cowboy with something firm and sturdy between his legs."

I roll my eyes. "I hate to break it to you, but the last time I checked, there's no rodeo in Halcyon Lake."

"Babe, it's rodeo season in South Dakota. The Stampede is next weekend!" She squeals.

"The Stampede?"

"Are you for real? You've never heard of the Corn Palace Stampede? Oh, you are in for the time of your life."

"Hannah, I can't go to South Dakota."

"Yes, you can. My cousin can hook us up with tickets, and we can stay at the campground. This is perfect. Just what you need!"

I shake my head. "My parents will never let me go."

"Sure they will! We'll get Dustin to drive us. And we'll invite your boy Simon—your mom and dad like him, right?

With two strong men to protect us, how can your parents say no?"

"Do you honestly think they'll let me go to South Dakota with you and two guys we barely know?"

"It's worth a shot, isn't it?" She grins.

When Hannah gets an idea in her head, especially a crazy one like this, there's no stopping her. I only knew her a few weeks when she convinced me that the best place to watch the Homecoming game was from the platform of the old water tower, even though she knew I was afraid of heights. She was right, and we had a great night until it was time to come down and I could hardly move. I was so terrified, dizzy.

"Isn't it?" she says again.

I'm exhausted. She sets her empty cup on the end table and sits on the sofa next to me. She loops her arm through mine and reaches for the remote.

"Let's watch a movie. It will take your mind off things." She flips through the channels until she finds an old Meg Ryan movie with a happy ending. "This will cheer you up, I promise."

My heart swells with love for her. We've only been friends since the beginning of the school year, but I love her. She's not Trixie—I will never have another friend like Trixie—but she's Hannah, and she's unique and loud and crass and she cares about my broken heart.

"Thanks," I whisper. "For everything."

She squeezes my arm. "Anything for you, Lucille."

29 · Ben

You've got to be kidding.

I've been lucky this summer, except for that one time, that Lucy hasn't been at the Full Loon on Monday nights.

But tonight when I walk in, catching the red screen door with my foot so it doesn't slam, I see her. I stop dead right there and my stomach lurches, like I'm still hungover from all that tequila, which is probably the case.

She's at a table in the far corner with Simon, and he's got this big grin on his face. He reaches across the table and runs his finger across the back of her hand. She smiles at him.

No. She should be with me. All the time, not just at a wedding.

No. Whatever. Her life. Her decision.

In a split second, I have to decide if I'm going to stay or go. My foot is in the door. I could turn and go out and no one would ever know I was there.

"Ben," Daniel calls from behind the counter. "You want your usual?"

Lucy looks up and her eyes bore into mine, her smile fades. I'm frozen. I can't move. Shit.

And it's like something has taken over my body when I shake my head in Daniel's direction. "No, I just remembered—"

I'm gone. I turn and I'm out the door, and I don't care who saw me and who didn't, but I will not sit there and eat a burger in front of Lucy and her douchebag boyfriend. Again.

Guthrie is in the parking lot.

"Hey, man," he says. "You going in?"

I shake my head.

"You okay? You look like you've seen a ghost."

"Yeah, fine," I say.

But I'm not fine. I'm angry. The rage courses through me, my heart pumping poison instead of blood. I could beat the shit out of Guthrie right now. I could beat the shit out of Simon. I could beat the shit out of me.

"You leaving?" he asks.

"Yeah, I gotta go."

He nods. "Okay, let's go. I'll drive. You can get pants-shitting drunk and pass out on the couch in my basement."

The way he says it, so serious, all the tension I feel disappears. I laugh and follow him to his car.

We drive out to his house, and his mom makes us macaroni and cheese. I don't get pants-shitting drunk. I don't drink at all. I have to work in the morning and there's nothing quite like the glare of the sun off the lake when you've got a hangover.

Especially when I've still got one from Saturday night.

Later, while Guthrie builds a fire in the pit, I decide to call Dana. I walk down to the lake.

I'm going to tell her that I think we should break up. I've

been working up to it since Lucy put her arm through mine at the church. Besides, I'm a shit boyfriend and she deserves someone better.

It's quiet on the shore, except for the bullfrogs, not like when I sit at the dock at Apple Tree Lane and can hear every car on Main Street. There's a pile of rocks next to the dock. I stack one on top of the other. It's not easy, and the rocks spill again and again, but I crave the repetition.

Dana picks up on the first ring. "Is everything okay? Aren't you with Guthrie? It's Monday."

"Yeah," I tell her.

"Are you drunk?"

"Nope."

I put another rock on top of the stack but it's not flat enough, and the whole thing falls over.

"Seriously, Ben, what's wrong?"

I fucking chicken out.

"I called to tell you good night," I say.

Dead silence.

"Dana?"

She clears her throat. "Good night, Ben. I love you."

I end the call. I toss my phone aside and restack the rocks, this time more carefully, more strategically. I get up and walk along the shore to find more stones and fill the pockets of my cargo shorts. I build another tower.

The stones of this one are irregular. The tower's off-balance, and the stack topples, knocking into the first one I made.

"Fuck," I mumble.

So I start over, switching out one rock for another, trying again when the towers tumble, until I've balanced the last stone.

I let out a long breath.

"Hey." Guthrie is behind me. I turn to face him. *"You are on the right path,"* he says.

"What?"

"Those look like inuksuit. One of the meanings of inuksuit is 'You are on the right path.' A marker. It's a way to let others know that you've been here, that this is the right path."

"Oh," I say. "Right."

We go back to the fire and Guthrie rattles on about this new hot spot he found on Papyrus, but I can't stop thinking about what he said.

You are on the right path.

Nothing feels right.

30 · *Lucy*

TUESDAY NIGHT, I GET UP ENOUGH COURAGE TO ASK MY dad about the rodeo. My mom's still at work. I figure it will be easier to convince Dad without her around, and then he can convince her.

Hannah comes with me. "Moral support," she says. "How can he say no when I'm standing right here?"

I'm pretty sure seeing Hannah in her miniscule tank top and skimpy, frayed cutoffs might have the opposite effect.

I raise my eyebrows. "Are you serious? Maybe you should put on some clothes first."

She rolls her eyes. "Your dad loves me."

I snort.

Dad's at the kitchen table with the paper and a cup of coffee.

"Hey." I sit down across from him. Hannah stands in the doorway.

"Hi, Luce." He nods in Hannah's direction. "Hannah."

"Hey, Mr. Meadows," Hannah says with an extra splash of twang.

There's no point in prolonging this. "Dad," I say, "Hannah's invited me to go to the Stampede in Mitchell this weekend."

He looks from me to Hannah and back to me. "That's the rodeo?"

"Yes."

"With her parents?"

"No, sir," Hannah pipes in. "With Dustin and Simon."

The boys were more than on board when Hannah mentioned a road trip.

"No, I'm afraid not."

Exactly what I was expecting.

"Dad, listen—"

"No, Lucy. You are sixteen years old. You're not old enough to go away for the weekend without an adult."

"Dustin's eighteen," Hannah offers, but my dad turns to glare at her, and she mumbles something about waiting outside before she disappears. So much for moral support.

"Dad, it's not like that."

"It's not like what?"

"I don't know, like *that*. Whatever you think. You automatically assume we're going to get in trouble or get pregnant or something. We're just going to go camping and see the rodeo, that's all. Two tents. Girls and boys. I swear."

"Sounds like you've got this all planned out."

"It was Simon's idea," I say. The lie slips out without a thought, and for a minute, I think it might work. Since that fishing trip on Father's Day when they bonded over Bond, my dad thinks Simon can do no wrong.

"The answer is no, Lucy."

"Dad, please," I can't keep the pleading out of my voice. "I don't ask for much. I want to get away for a weekend."

He interrupts me. "You just spent a weekend in Duluth. How much more time away do you need?"

If he only knew. "I was *working*. Isn't this what you wanted, for me to spend more time with friends? I promise, nothing will happen. And it's *Simon*. Don't you trust him?"

"I don't trust him enough for you to go away for the weekend with him. We don't know him."

"I know him," I say, and bite my lip.

He looks at me with a tilt of his head and his eyes narrow.

"How well do you know him, Lucy? You two have been seeing a lot of each other lately, haven't you?"

I nod. "Yes. We're *dating*, Dad. It's not a crime."

"No," he says again. "You're not going to South Dakota with a boy we hardly know."

"You know him! He's been living next door all summer!"

"Lucy—"

"You would let Clayton go."

"That's different."

Of course it's different. It's different to him but not to me. Clayton at sixteen? He would have loved to raise hell at a rodeo.

"Nice double standard, Dad." My words are sharp, bitter.

I don't wait to hear his reply, if he has one. I turn and am out of the kitchen in a flash. I head to the front porch where Hannah waits.

"We're going," I tell her. "I don't care what he says, and I'm not even going to bother asking my mom. We're going."

"Yeehaw!" Hannah whoops and throws her pink cowgirl hat high into the air.

Sneaking out of the house Friday night is almost too easy. I stay up later than my parents, watching TV. I turn the volume down, set the timer for it to power off at 12:30, and slip out the front door a few minutes before midnight. I don't bother to leave a note. They'll figure it out soon enough.

I walk down our long driveway, where Dustin will have parked his truck. Simon will meet us there, too, although he's going to South Dakota with his mother's blessing, since she's got an art fair in St. Paul this weekend. She told him to have a great time, that she was proud of him for broadening his horizons.

Dustin's enormous red pickup is parked on the shoulder. Hannah's with him, and of course they're making out. She sits on the open tailgate, her legs wrapped around him.

I don't see Simon. I clear my throat.

Dustin turns his head but keeps his arms around Hannah's waist.

"Hey, Lucy," he says, and grins. "All set?"

"Yep." I shove my duffel bag into the covered bed next to Hannah. Simon shows up with a backpack and a plastic bag full of convenience-store snacks.

He pulls me close and kisses me hard. "This is going to be a weekend we'll never forget," he whispers.

The drive to Mitchell is seven long hours. Hannah promises

to stay awake to keep Dustin company while he drives, but I'm tired. My knees are smashed against Hannah's seat back, my cheek against the cold window. There's a crick in my neck.

"Lucy," Simon says after a while, "that can't be comfortable."

He pulls me toward him. He's warm. His shoulder, his smell, have become familiar. He wraps an arm around me and I fall asleep there.

31 · Ben

GUTHRIE AND I ARE OUT IN THE BACKYARD AT THE FIRE PIT when I get the text from Tami.

Have you seen Lucy today? No one has seen or heard from her since last night.

My first thought is, *Why is Tami asking me? How the hell would I know?* But then my stomach heaves.

Lucy is missing. I hit *call.*

"Tami," I say when she picks up, "what do you mean no one has heard from her?"

"Daniel called." She sounds worried. "Lucy's parents are flipping out. They thought she was here today, but when she didn't come home for dinner, her dad tried to call her. It went straight to voicemail. Same with Hannah's phone. Have you seen either of them today?"

"No." My stomach twists again. I don't know what I'll do if something happened to Lucy, too. "I'll call you back if I find out anything." I stand up and pace back and forth in front of the fire.

"What's up?" Guthrie asks.

"Lucy. She's missing."

Guthrie takes a swig from his bottle of water. "She's not missing. Everyone knows she went to South Dakota with Hannah and Dustin and Simon."

Fuck.

"What? How do you know?"

"Hannah told me Lucy's parents wouldn't let her go to the rodeo this weekend, but they were going to go anyway."

"When did you see Hannah?"

"I see her around," he says.

I sit back down and call Tami again.

"You should ask Lucy's mom and dad if they know of any reason she might have gone to South Dakota for the weekend." I hang up before Tami can say anything.

"Dude, you need another beer," Guthrie says and hands me an ice-cold bottle from the cooler at his feet. The glass feels good in my hot, sweaty hand. The beer feels even better as it chills and numbs my throat. I want to be numb.

Numb is better than the feeling of worry that crept deep into me and twisted my insides. For thirty seconds, tops, I thought something had happened to Lucy. Those thirty seconds felt like the ceiling had crashed in, that the world had spun to a halt.

I remember that feeling.

The beer goes down easy. I throw my empty bottle on the ground by the cooler and stand up again.

"I gotta go," I say.

Guthrie shrugs. "Be careful, Ben."

"What the hell is that supposed to mean?"

"Get your shit together. Either you want to be with her or you don't, but make a decision and stop messing with people."

He stands up and waves as he walks toward the house. "In case you're wondering, the rodeo is in Mitchell. Mitchell, South Dakota."

There are a lot of reasons why Guthrie is my best friend, has been since second grade when we both got in trouble for hiding out in the woods behind school, trying to hit squirrels with a slingshot, instead of coming in after recess. Guthrie gets it.

I've had a couple of beers but don't feel a thing. I get in the car and send a text to Mum that I'm staying at Guthrie's tonight. I've got a full tank of gas and GPS on my cell and fuck-all, I'm going to drive to Mitchell, South Dakota.

I think about Lucy. I think about how much I've missed her, her laughter, her smile, and how, when I get to Mitchell, I'm finally going to get the balls to apologize.

I crank the radio loud to stay awake. For a while I even catch Darkness Radio out of the Twin Cities, talk radio about paranormal shit, and when the story of a mysterious unsolved murder in St. Cloud freaks me out too much, I switch over to a classical station and blast it.

I get to Marshall, a town on the western edge of Minnesota, close to the South Dakota border, and I stop to take a leak and get gas.

I've been driving three, maybe three and a half hours. I've got at least three more to go.

But I'm standing in front of the cooler in the gas station when suddenly it hits me.

I'm an idiot. I'm driving to Mitchell, South Dakota, to try to find my dead sister's best friend at a fucking rodeo. And she's there with another guy. And let's not forget that I've got a girlfriend. How stupid am I?

Pretty fucking stupid.

What would I say to her? How the hell would I even *find* her?

She wouldn't forgive me, anyway.

What I said was unforgiveable.

I am unforgiveable.

I buy a Coke and turn around.

Somewhere around Willmar, I start to cry. Not big, racking sobs like right after Trixie died, but these pools of tears that make it impossible to see, no matter how often I rub them away. It's ridiculous. I don't even know why I'm crying. I pull over at a park bordering a lake. I walk down to the beach, and my heart is pounding so hard, I feel like I can't breathe.

I drop down to my knees and sift through the sand and grass looking for good rocks, and then I remember the stones I found at Guthrie's that are in the pockets of my shorts. I stack the rocks, and the act of putting one stone on top of another calms me somehow.

I've stacked rocks everywhere. Next to the cracked concrete steps at the shack where we clean fish. In the grass at the edge of the parking lot at the bank. At the top of the Fire Tower.

And even though I promised myself I wouldn't go back to the cemetery, I stacked them on top of Trixie's gravestone, where I'd seen Lucy put the candy. The wind probably blew them down before I even got to my car, but it was enough that, for a few minutes at least, there was balance, and it soothed something inside of me, that constant ache.

Trixie would know what to do. She would know how I should ask Lucy for forgiveness.

But she's not here.

I stack the rocks and they fall and I stack them again until I find balance.

32 · Lucy

Mitchell, South Dakota, is hot, humid, and dusty. We're here plenty early so we wander around town, watch part of the parade, have lunch at a small-town diner not unlike the Full Loon Café. Simon orders a slice of coconut cream pie, and even though he practically licks the plate clean, declares that it's nowhere near as good as the pie at the Full Loon. Overheated and sweating, we set up our tents at the campground, then head over to the rodeo grounds.

I've never seen Hannah so happy, so at home, so relaxed. She's wearing a tight white T-shirt from another rodeo that says, "Put Something Exciting Between Your Legs." She shows us every nook and cranny of the rodeo. She flirts with cowboys and the guys grilling hamburgers. Dustin stands beside her, his hand on her back, and grins in his cretin way while she finagles down the price on a purple straw cowboy hat.

"Sweetheart, I *saw* you out back behind the trailer, colorin' this with purple *spray paint*," she says in a sweet voice. "Now, come on. This white one here is five dollars less. It's only a little spray paint, sugar—don't you want to sell me this for the same price?"

Apparently he does, and Hannah gets the hat for five dollars off.

I turn on my phone as we walk from Vendor Alley back to the stands. Eighteen missed calls, seven voicemail messages, most from my dad. Thirty-two text messages from Dad, Mom, Daniel, Tami, even one from Clayton. His is the only one I open.

Girl UR in deep shit. I've never been prouder.

I stumble and bite my bottom lip to stop its sudden tremble.

"You okay, Lucille?" Hannah says as she grabs my arm to steady me. "Trip over your own feet?"

"You might say that." I hold the phone out for her to see.

She laughs. "This will all blow over, you'll see."

We watch the Grand March and the first few events. Hannah whoops and hollers during barrel racing and steer wrestling.

Simon reaches for my hand. "Come on. Let's get out of here."

I shake my head. "Seriously? We came all this way to see a rodeo. Don't you want to, you know, see the rodeo?"

He smiles. "Nah, I came all this way to spend time with you. Don't you want to, *you know*, spend time with me?"

"Of course," I say. "We're spending time together now."

"I don't care about the rodeo, and I don't think you do, either. It's not your thing. I mean, look at Hannah. Look at how excited she is whenever some dude falls off a horse trying to rope a calf." He pauses, then says, "How about we, um, go back to the campground?"

I don't answer right away.

I'm here with Simon, who slipped into my life so easily. My boyfriend.

Ben doesn't want to be with me. He's made that clear, time and again.

Simon does.

"Yeah," I say finally, "let's go."

Hannah raises her eyebrows at me when we get up to leave. I shrug.

The walk back is brutal. It's about a hundred degrees, even at nine o'clock at night, and by the time we reach our tent, rivers of sweat drip down my back. It's cooler down by the lake at least. The campground is nearly deserted—everyone is still at the rodeo and will be for another couple of hours. I can hear the roar of the crowd and the tinny, twangy voice of the announcer from here.

We sit in the camp chairs outside the tent and watch the darkness fall over the lake. Simon gets up from his chair and kneels in front of me. He takes my hands in his.

"Having fun?"

I smile. I'm hot, sweaty, dusty. "Yeah. It's been fun."

"I always have fun with you, Lucy. It's been a great summer so far."

I nod. He stands and pulls me to my feet, into him, his chin on the top of my head.

"You're amazing, Lucy. You've made this such an awesome summer for me. I don't want to go home."

I can feel his heartbeat against my cheek, his T-shirt damp with sweat. "There's still a lot of summer left."

"Not enough," he murmurs.

The rumble of his voice, the thick air around us, the warmth of his arms—it all wraps around me, holds me tight.

This boy wants to be with me.

Simon kisses me and I kiss him back. He leads me into the tent. He guides me down to the sleeping bag, his weight heavy on top of me.

"Is this okay?" he asks. "I mean, we don't have to if you don't want to."

He's nervous.

Strangely, I'm not.

He asks again, "Is this okay?"

It is. I nod.

He says, "I love you, Lucy."

When I don't say anything, he continues. "No matter what, I love you. I had no idea what was in store for me this summer when my mom said we'd be renting some house up north. But now I know that I'm the luckiest guy on earth."

He kisses me, and it's sweet and gentle and I believe that he loves me.

I close my eyes. I tell myself that I'm moving on. I'm letting Ben go.

Simon holds my hand across the space between our two camp chairs outside the tent. The sky is deep bluish-black, the bright spotlights from the rodeo grounds visible in the distance. The cheering has died down, though, so Hannah and Dustin should be on their way back.

"Lucy, are you okay?" Simon sounds anxious, almost

uncomfortable, asking me this. We weren't in the tent long, and I was grateful when he gave me privacy after, to clean up and get dressed.

"Yes." I feel strange, thinned out. But it's okay.

"Okay." He lets out a long breath. "Good."

When I don't respond, he changes the subject. "I've always wanted to see the Corn Palace. You think we'll have time tomorrow?"

The World's Only Corn Palace is a big tourist attraction in town, decorated each year in a design made of more than a quarter of a million ears of corn.

"Maybe."

"Don't you think it's fascinating? I mean, for one, think of the effort it must take to grow all that corn—all those different colors—and then to actually nail it to the wall. It's a work of art." He smiles. "You want to go?"

A loud whoop comes from a couple sites down, and I look up to see Hannah and Dustin. Dustin carries a bundle of firewood.

"You missed the big finale!" Hannah winks at me. "How are you two lovebirds?"

The heat rushes over my face.

"Never better." Simon's voice cracks and he reaches for a bottle of water.

"Let's make a fire," Dustin says. "I'll teach you how, city boy."

• • •

After the fire burns down, Hannah insists that she and I sleep in one tent, the boys in the other. This is a surprise to everyone, even me.

"Come on, babe," Dustin says, his hands on her butt. He squeezes. "You're kidding, right?"

She shakes her head and gives Dustin a playful shove. "Her parents would kill me."

They'll probably kill me first.

The embers hiss as Dustin pours water over them. He takes off his cowboy hat, kisses Hannah, and ducks into the tent. Simon pulls me to my feet and hugs me.

"Good night, Lucy," he whispers into my ear. "I love you."

He follows Dustin into the tent.

Hannah unzips the opening of our tent, holds it back for me, and follows me in.

"You want to talk about anything?" she asks. She's curled up the edges of her purple crocheted cowboy hat. She takes it off and swats it against my arm. She smiles. Beautiful Hannah, always happy.

I nod. "But not yet. Not when they might hear us."

I barely sleep in the heat and humidity. I toss and turn and wait for morning.

33 · Ben

Mum's all over me in the morning. "Ben, you look terrible. What's wrong? Are you ill?"

I don't know. I didn't sleep. I drove all night and sat in my car in Guthrie's driveway until I figured it was late enough to go home.

Lucy shouldn't be dating that guy. But it's not like I think she should be with me, right, so I'm not really entitled to that opinion.

Except I am.

She shouldn't be dating that guy.

Mum sets a mug of hot coffee in front of me. "Tami told me about Lucy. Did you know anything about this?"

The coffee is scorching hot, but it's what I need. I hope it will burn, destroy everything that's killing me from the inside right now. I shouldn't feel like this. I pushed Lucy away a long time ago.

"Ben? Did you hear me?"

I shake my head and stand up. "I have to go. I'm supposed to be at the resort."

"You're off today," Mum says. "Please stay. I want to talk to you."

"Emily asked me to take her fishing." I walk across the kitchen, open the screen door to the garage, and let it slam behind me.

• • •

The sun is so bright and blue, bluebird skies. A perfect, sunny summer day, but not so great for catching fish. Emily won't know the difference. She's thrilled that I want to take her fishing.

I drive to the resort and find Emily and Tami at the table on the deck, the umbrella shading them from the bright sun. Emily's coloring.

"Hey, Em, you ready to go fishing?"

Emily jumps up from her chair and bounces. "Yes, yes, yes!"

"Fishing?" Tami asks.

"See? I told you Ben was going to take me fishing today!" Emily shouts.

"But—" Tami starts, then pauses. "I thought you weren't comfortable taking Emily out on the boat."

"I don't want to talk about it," I say.

She's quiet for a minute, and then says, "Thanks for the tip about the rodeo."

"I don't want to talk about it."

Emily saves me. She stops bouncing and tugs on my hand instead. "C'mon, Ben, let's go!"

She pulls me down the hill to the boat.

I'm wrecked, tired as hell, but I'm going to help Emily catch some fish.

I take us to a quiet, shady spot on the lake, not too weedy, so she won't get her line tangled. She's spinning her chair in the bow, watching her bobber.

"Ben," she says, "why didn't you go to the rodeo with Lucy?"

"I wasn't invited," I tell her. Simple enough. How does she know about the rodeo anyway?

"I'm going to get married," she says, an abrupt change of topic. I'm used to it by now. She hasn't stopped talking about weddings and brides and dresses since we got back from Duluth.

"Really?"

"Yes, someday," she says. "Can I marry you?"

I smile. "Nope. I'm your cousin. You can't marry someone who is related to you."

She thinks about this for a minute. "Is Lucy related?"

"You want to marry Lucy?"

She laughs. "No, I don't want to marry Lucy. *You* should marry Lucy. If we're not related to her."

I'm surprised at how tight my chest feels. "No, we're not related."

"Well?"

"Well, what?"

"Well, will you marry her?"

I take a deep breath. I had hoped for an easy day of fishing and instead I get barraged with questions about weddings. And Lucy.

"Well, it's complicated."

"Oh, I know what that means. Lucy explained it to me. Complicated is like when all the pieces of the puzzle don't come together right."

I nod. "That sounds about right. Lucy's pretty smart."

Emily grins. "I know. Which is why you should marry her. Will you tell me a *Trixie*?"

"What do you mean, Em? What's a *Trixie*?" My throat is tight.

"A *Trixie*. A story about her. Lucy tells them."

"Oh." I'm not sure how to respond. "Lucy tells you stories about Trix?"

"Yeah. You can, too. It's easy. I'll start for you. *Once upon a time, there was a little girl named Beatrix, but everyone called her Trixie. She was smart and sweet and nice to everyone. She had a best friend named Lulu and a brother named Ben. One day . . .*"

She stops and looks at me. "Well, it's your turn now. *One day . . .*"

"Oh," I say again. "Okay. One day—well, night, really—Trixie and her friend Lulu took the rowboat out—"

Emily cuts me off. "I know this one! This is the one where Trixie drops the oar in, right, and you come out and rescue them?"

I swallow hard. When will this pain in my chest ease?

Emily's bobber goes under and she squeals. "Help me!" she cries, and she forgets about the story.

I don't.

34 · Lucy

WHEN HANNAH WAKES, I'M ALREADY PACKED.

"Let's go for a walk," she says, pulling on shorts and a T-shirt and her purple hat. "I'm starving!"

We walk to the campground convenience store, buy coffee and breakfast sandwiches, and find a picnic table close to the lake.

"So, how was it?" Hannah asks after she downs her first coffee and starts on the second.

I blush. "How was it supposed to be?"

She laughs. "That good, huh? Tell me he used a condom."

I nod.

"Well, that's a relief. Makes you wonder, though."

"Yeah. Kinda presumptuous."

"You know he's going to want it all the time now," she says. She laughs again, then grows serious. "Do you—I don't know, do you regret it?"

I shake my head. "No. I wanted to do it. I wouldn't have if I didn't want to."

"But?"

"He's so sweet. He makes me feel like I'm something special, you know? It's just . . ." I pause, and then, "It's not his fault that he's not who I want him to be."

There's a long moment when neither of us speaks. I wanted being with Simon to mean getting over Ben.

A chill washes over me.

I don't know that I'll ever get over Ben.

"What do you love about Ben? I mean, I didn't know him before, but he seems like a moody little prick, if you ask me."

"He wasn't always like that, you know."

"So you've said."

I don't even know where to begin. Why do I love Ben? Why do I breathe? Why do I eat? And then I remember that first day I told Trixie, and the first five things I loved about him.

"Well . . ." I say slowly. "I love that when he laughs really hard, he gets this one little dimple on the right side."

Hannah looks at me and rolls her eyes. "I have never seen Ben laugh really hard. Scowl, yes. Laugh, no."

"He used to laugh all the time."

"Before," she says, her tone sad.

"Before."

"What else? There's got to be more than a dimple that is clearly an urban legend."

"Funny. You know about the agates, how he used to polish rocks?" I slip my hand into my pocket to make sure the agate is there and startle when I remember that it's not. "I don't think he does it anymore. But when he did, he was always so careful and gentle with the stones. Like they were the most precious things on earth. And I always thought that he treated people the same way he handled the rocks. He cared."

"'Cared' as in past tense?" Hannah asks. "Again, this is not something I've witnessed."

"I know."

"What else?"

"He calls his mother Mum."

"Weird."

"She's British. Emily was the first baby he ever held. She was so tiny in his arms, and he held her so carefully, like she might break. I remember everything about the day she was born. I got to go to the hospital with them to visit. He looked down at her and grinned, like he'd never seen anything so amazing in his life."

"That's so sweet," Hannah says.

I nod. "Emily has always felt so safe around Ben. He's strong and smart and he knows how to take care of people. And I guess that's what I loved most about him. He made me feel safe, like if I was with him, nothing bad would happen."

"But it did," Hannah says, slowly, cautiously. "And he hasn't been very protective of you since, has he?"

She's right again. I nod. "He's changed."

"Yeah, he's changed, but it doesn't mean that deep down, everything you loved about him isn't still there."

Maybe. Maybe it is. But I've changed, too.

"So that's it?" Hannah says in a light tone when I don't say anything. "That's what you love about him so much? How about those abs or that cute butt?" She grins.

"Oh, there's more. But Trixie asked me what I liked about him right after I confessed to her. Those were the first five things I thought of."

"And you remember them? After all this time?"

"I'll never forget."

"I wish I had known Trixie," Hannah says. "Do you think all three of us would have been friends? Or maybe you wouldn't have needed me, and I would have been the lonely new girl."

"Oh, I think Trix would have loved you," I say, and I mean it.

"Tell me about her," Hannah says.

I do. I tell her all my best *Trixies.*

I tell her about swim meets and sleepovers and shopping trips to St. Cloud for new school clothes. I tell her about summer days on the pontoon, summer evenings at the Watermelon Days carnival.

Someday I will tell this story to Emily, how Hannah and I sat at this picnic table and talked about Trixie, and this memory will be one of my best *Hannahs.*

"I suppose we should get back to the boys," I say.

I'm surprised when Hannah hugs me.

"I know I tease you about Ben a lot, but it's *obvious,* Lucille. You shouldn't be hooking up with Simon Stanford. You and Ben should be together. I'm serious. Anybody can see it."

"That's sweet, but I think we both know that is not going to happen."

"You don't know that it won't happen with Ben. Miracles happen every day. You have to believe it in your heart."

"I don't believe in miracles." Not since that day on the beach when I prayed for a miracle that didn't come.

"Aw, honey." She stands and brushes crumbs off her shirt. "Don't let this bring you down. Come on, let's go home and face *that* music."

"Thanks. I don't know what I'd do without you, Hannah."

"You know I got you, Lucille." She squeezes my hand and we walk back to our campsite.

Dustin stops the truck at the side of the road, doesn't even bother to pull into the driveway. Simon gets out and unloads our bags from the back. He hands me my duffel but doesn't let go, not right away, and his hand grazes mine.

"Hey," he says, his eyes locked on mine, "it's okay, Luce. Everything is going to be okay."

I pinch my lips together in a grim smile. "I hope so."

We walk up to the driveway. He leans in, kisses me on the cheek, and says hello to my dad, who is waiting on the front porch.

"Mr. Meadows," he says, and nods. Like we hadn't just sneaked off to a rodeo without his permission and had sex in a tent.

Dad ignores Simon and pulls me into a tight, quick hug, then nearly pushes me away. "Lucy, how could you? How could you do this?"

I don't know how to answer that. I look back at Simon, who mouths, "Call me later," and disappears down the other side of the driveway.

"I'm sorry," I tell Dad. There's nothing else. There's no reasonable excuse, no way to explain it away. I follow Dad into the house.

Mom sits at the kitchen table, a cup of coffee in front of her that looks untouched.

She's not at the restaurant. She's here, waiting for me, her daughter, to come home. I wonder who's covering my shift.

"Mom." I take a tentative step forward. "Mom, I'm so sorry. I shouldn't have worried you like that."

The look of sadness and concern in her eyes when she looks up from her cup of coffee stops me cold.

"What has gotten into you, Lucy?" she asks, her voice cracking. "You've never acted this way before. You've never disobeyed us. Your dad tells you that you can't go to South Dakota, and the next thing we know, you're sneaking off in the middle of the night."

When she pauses, Dad starts in. "You should not have gone to that rodeo. We were worried sick. So it should be no surprise that you're grounded for the rest of the summer. You can go to work at the resort and the diner and that's it. And you will not be allowed to see any of your friends."

"No," I cry. "You have to let me see Hannah. Please—"

Mom cuts me off. "You made your choice, Lucy, and now you've got to live with the consequences. End of discussion."

I turn and run up the stairs, away from my parents.

I shower and crawl into bed, but I don't fall asleep for a long time. I send Hannah a text to make sure everything's all right and her text back is that she's tired, she's worried about me, she'll talk to me tomorrow.

The murmurs of my mom and dad carry upstairs through the vents. Their anger and disappointment tear at me. I'm sorry that I went to South Dakota and I'm not sorry.

My mother's words echo in my mind.

You made your choice, and now you've got to live with the consequences.

35 · Ben

A COUPLE OF DAYS AFTER LUCY GETS BACK FROM THE RODEO, Tami takes Emily to Brainerd for a doctor's appointment, so Lucy's shift is all resort work. I heard from Guthrie who heard from Hannah that she's grounded, only allowed to go to work. That she can't even see Hannah. Or Simon.

There's a small part of me that's happy about it, the part about Simon, at least.

And there's another part of me, a bigger one, that's pissed at her and Hannah for going to that rodeo in the first place. But why should I be pissed about it? What right do I have?

Which pisses me off even more—at myself.

I watch as Lucy scoops goose poop off the beach and lawn. She fills bird feeders and puts fresh water in the birdbaths, cleans the fish house, even chops firewood.

I've been helping out around Apple Tree Lane for years, tagging along beside my dad and uncle, fishing, raking the beach. It's never felt like work. There's something about the hum of a boat motor, the shimmer of the midafternoon sun on the surface of the water, the cool breeze off the lake on a hot day.

Whoever named this lake couldn't have chosen better. Halcyon Lake. Idyllic. Untroubled. Peaceful.

Until your sister dies swimming to the island.

But the landscape doesn't care that my world changed that day. The lake and the jack pines and the breeze carry on like nothing's different. Somehow we're all supposed to carry on, too—my parents and me and Lucy and everyone who loved Trixie.

At three o'clock, Lucy starts the garbage run, driving the UTV around to pick up the bags of trash guests leave outside their cabins. From the dock, where I'm getting the boat ready for my next fishing trip at four, I hear a sputter and a high-pitched whine, then the engine dies.

I wait for a minute to see if John will come out of the lodge to help. He doesn't. Lucy turns the key and hits the start button, tries to get it going again, but the engine doesn't turn over. Then she gets out of the driver's seat and kicks one of the tires.

Shit.

I walk up to where she's stalled, in front of Loon. She's red-faced and sweaty. She looks down, scratches a line in the gravel with the toe of her tennis shoe.

"I don't need your help," she snaps.

She used to let me help her. The time she and Trixie took the rowboat and lost the oar. The time Trixie dared Lu to climb the tallest tree at Sullivan Street Park and she couldn't get down. I climbed up, too, and talked her the whole way down, one shaky step at a time.

She used to trust me.

I didn't used to be such a dick.

"Let me take a look," I say.

She takes a step back, then another, giving me plenty of room to move around the utility vehicle.

I slide into the driver's seat, turn the key, flip the kill switch, and press the start button. Nothing. I glance at her, but she's got her back to me, facing the lake.

I push down the brake, try it again, and there's a sputter. I adjust the choke and the thing fires. She looks at me then, and I wonder if she's about to smile, but she does the opposite. Her brows furrow together.

"Um, thanks," she says, "but what if—"

"You want me to finish the run?" I ask. Slow, tentative, not sure how she'll react. I want to do something nice for her, even if it's just picking up garbage.

She looks at me for a long time, like she's trying to figure out if she should let me help her, or if she's going to be stubborn and tell me to shove off. She should tell me to shove off. I deserve it. Seconds tick by, and I'm worried that if she doesn't make a decision soon, I'll be late for my fishing trip.

"You drive," she says. "I'll ride along and pick up the garbage."

I take a chance and smile at her. She doesn't smile back.

She gets in, and I drive her to the next cabin and the next. She doesn't say a word. I take her up to the Dumpsters behind the lodge and get out to help her toss in the bags. Still she doesn't say anything, and I don't, either.

What should I say? That I'm sorry?

There's too much to be sorry for.

It's not until after I've driven the UTV back down to the utility shed and she's climbed out that she says, "Thanks for your help, Ben."

It's nothing, it's so stupid, but my heart fills up when I hear her say my name.

36 · Lucy

THE TERMS OF MY PRISON SENTENCE ALLOW ME TO GO TO Apple Tree Lane and the Full Loon. Nowhere else. For four weeks, until school starts. I'm okay with it, except that I don't get to see Hannah. Simon sends texts and leaves voicemail messages while I'm at work: *Can't wait till u can kick my ass at mini golf again. Miss u. Any chance u can bring me a slice of 5 layer chocolate?*

He'll leave for the summer before my sentence is up. There won't be any more mini-golf. I can't say that I'll miss it. Him.

One afternoon, my parents both at work, I take a chance and walk into town for a few books at the used bookstore.

Mom and I used to love coming to the Broken Spine. "We'll just pop in for a minute," she'd say, "to see if there's anything we can't live without."

We couldn't live without a complete set of the Little House books, which she read to me the winter of second grade, or the Betsy-Tacy books, set in a town in southern Minnesota. We couldn't live without *Kneeknock Rise* and *The Search for Delicious*. Of course we couldn't live without Harry Potter.

After I buy a few books, I step through the open doorway between the Broken Spine and Sweet Pea's. I love the combination of the musty bookstore and the sugary sweetness of the candy shop.

I stand at the fudge display for a long time. They've added new flavors since I was here last—maple bacon and white-chocolate cake batter and salted caramel.

"Hey, Lucy," Mrs. Stewart says when she sees me at the counter. "What can I get for you?"

I ask for my family's favorites: peanut butter, rocky road, mint chocolate chip, maple.

I think about the last time I bought fudge for Ben, the week before Trixie died.

"It's a sign, you know," she'd said as we left the store to walk back to her house. "That you and Ben both love maple fudge."

A sign. I laughed and Trixie swatted me on the arm.

"You laugh now," she said, "but just you wait and see."

"Sorry," I tell Mrs. Stewart now, "can you make that two maples instead of the mint chocolate chip?"

I furrow my brow. I think I just bought fudge for Ben. I don't know why I would buy fudge for someone who's hurt me. But I do it.

My phone buzzes with a text as I pay. It's from Simon: *Break out of prison today?*

How did he know?

What do you mean? I send back.

Why r u at Sweet P's? ;) I'm across the street.

I step outside into the sunshine with my bag of used paperbacks and box of fudge. Simon meets me on the sidewalk and reaches for the bag from the bookstore. His tan is deeper, dark against his Dr Pepper T-shirt, the one he was wearing the first

day we met. He smiles, a slow, lazy grin that's become so familiar the last few weeks. It's the first time I've seen him since
South Dakota. He's still my boyfriend.

I can't help but think of the extra piece of maple fudge,
wrapped in light green tissue.

He reaches out and touches the brim of my Twins baseball cap, pulled low on my forehead. "Your clever disguise isn't
working. I'd recognize you anywhere."

"What are you doing here?" I try to smile.

"I should ask *you* that! Sneaking off to buy—what's in this
bag?"

"From the bookstore? Books."

He opens the bag and pulls out the books. "*Wuthering
Heights. The House of Mirth. The Awakening.* Light summer
reading or what?" He slips them back into the bag.

"Well, I have a lot of extra time on my hands now."

"Yeah," he says, "sorry about that. What did you buy at
Sweet Pea's?"

"Fudge."

"Ooh." He takes the box and sniffs. "Maple? Do I smell
maple?"

I grab the box back.

"Whoa, this must be pretty good fudge. Who's it for?"

"No one. My family." My words are sharper than I intended,
but he must not notice.

"Lucy, I've really missed you."

I nod and reach for my books. "I've missed you, too. But I

should get going. I need to get back home before anyone else sees me."

Simon tucks the bag under his arm and reaches for my hand. "I'll give you a ride, okay?"

No. No, it's not okay. Not today, when I've just bought maple fudge for Ben.

"Oh, no," I say, "it's fine. You must have other things you'd rather do."

"Nope. I want to, Lucy, really. I was headed home anyway."

He's so nice about it, so earnest.

"Well," I say. "I guess."

That's when I see him—Ben, coming out of the drugstore, a plastic bag in each fist.

He pauses when he sees us, but only for a second. Without thinking, I drop Simon's hand.

"Lucy, you okay?" Simon asks, and then, "Oh."

Ben nods at us and walks around the side of the building to the parking lot.

That's why I hadn't noticed the Firebird.

Simon is talking to me, but I have no idea what he's said. "What?"

"I asked if there's a reason you don't want Ben to see us holding hands?" His tone is crisp, but there's hurt there, too.

I don't have an answer. There are too many reasons.

But I don't want to hurt him.

"Oh, shoot." I reach up on my tiptoes to kiss his cheek. "There's someplace else I need to go. Don't wait."

"Where? Won't you get in more trouble if you get caught?"

I ignore that question, too. "Mom brought home some caramel pecan rolls last night. I'll try to sneak one over later, okay?"

I take the box of fudge from him and walk away before he can say anything else.

I cut through the woods behind Goldilocks to the trail that leads to Sullivan Street Park. It's safer than walking through town and risking being seen by my mom or someone who'll tell her they saw me. It's cooler here under the shade of the trees, but it's still humid and, with my quick pace, I'm sweating and breathing heavily in no time. I stop at a bench, sit down, and take a long drink from my water bottle with my eyes closed.

When I open them again, I see a stack of rocks on the shore at the base of a birch tree—the largest one at the bottom the size of a bowling ball. I think about how we tried to stack rocks at Lake Superior last year, how my towers and Trixie's toppled and we laughed, but Ben—Ben was so careful and methodical about it, so intent on achieving balance where there should be none.

I could stay here at the park for the rest of the day, at home among the trees, a cool breeze coming off the lake. But I've wasted too much time here, and I'm worried that Dad will get home before I do. I pull my cap down lower on my forehead, cross the parking lot, and head for home.

37 · Ben

I'M RAKING THE WEEDS OFF THE SWIMMING BEACH AFTER
lunch when Dad corners me.

"When you're done there," he says, "we've got to level off
the dock down by Bear."

"Sure," I tell him. I don't look up from the wet sand of the
shoreline, but I'm glad for the distraction. I've been thinking
about Lucy again. I've been thinking about her since I saw her
and her boyfriend when I was at the drugstore the other day.
I've been thinking about her all summer, to be honest.

It's hot today, and I'd rather be out on the lake fishing than
doing all this resort maintenance. At least I'll be able to stand
in the lake and cool off when we work on the dock.

"And don't forget," Dad continues, "tonight we're taking
Mum out to the Twenty-Seven Club for her birthday."

"Yep."

He's quiet for a minute; I can feel his eyes on me. Then:
"You think you can sober up long enough to take your mother
out for a nice dinner?"

I snap my head up and glare at him. "You think you can?"

Dad shakes his head. "What has gotten into you, Ben? Be
angry at me, I don't care. But don't take this—whatever this
is—out on your mum. She doesn't deserve it."

"Whatever this is?"

He waves his hand in front of me. "Your attitude. You think

you're the only one in this family who's hurting? Jesus, Ben, think about somebody other than yourself for once."

He turns and walks up the hill. He's right, I know he's right. I've been a selfish bastard since Trixie died, but I don't know how else to handle it. I can't deal with it the way they want me to. Put fresh flowers in Trixie's room. Pray for her soul on Sundays. Shit, I can't even do what Lucy does when she sits up at Trixie's grave, talking to her, leaving her candy. I guess being an asshole is the only way.

Toward the end of my shift, I go up to the lodge, where Emily is sitting at the counter with a glass of milk and a piece of fudge. I recognize the green tissue paper it rests on.

"Whatcha got there, Emily?" I ask.

"Lucy bought me fudge," she says. "It's maple. Want to try some?"

A few seconds pass before I can bring myself to answer. Something inside of me tightens when I think of the pieces of fudge Lucy used to leave for me on Saturday mornings.

I never thanked her.

For one crazy second, I think that once Emily's done with the fudge, I'll offer to throw away the tissue. Instead, I'll slip it into my pocket and keep it there like Lucy keeps the agate I gave her.

And then I snap out of it.

"That's great," I tell her. When she's finished, I take the green wrapper, crumple it in my fist, and throw it in the trash.

• • •

The Twenty-Seven Club is this old supper club out on County Road 27, Mum's favorite restaurant for surf and turf. The wide bank of windows overlooks Story Lake on one side and the golf course on the other. Dad reserved a table on the lake side, a huge bouquet of gerbera daisies, her favorite flower, in the center.

"Welcome to the Twenty-Seven Club, where the only thing we overlook is Story Lake," the hostess says. We've heard it a million times. She hands us menus, even though we all order the same thing every time.

"Lovely flowers," Mum says.

After the hostess has left with our drink orders, Bess, one of the owners, steps over to our table. "Haven't seen you folks in a while. How are you, dear?" she says to Mum, a look of pity crossing her face.

God, even here. We can't get away from it, almost a year later.

"Just fine," Mum says. "My boys are treating me to a lovely dinner for my birthday. And it's just lovely to see you, Bess."

Mum's anxious; I can tell by the way she said *lovely* so many times.

Saturday nights at the supper club were a big deal when Trixie and I were younger—we'd dress up in our church clothes and act like grown-ups, clinking our water goblets together and saying *cheers* in British accents like Mum, over and over.

A couple of years ago I noticed that the tables were scuffed, the upholstery sticky, the famous line about overlooking Story

Lake worn out. The magic of the supper club faded. And that's how I feel tonight, with my faded, sad parents across the table from me, the seat next to me where Trixie should be, empty.

We order—surf and turf for both Mum and Dad and a rack of ribs for me. Trix always ordered the Twenty-Seven Shrimp Special and brought the leftovers home to share.

Mum folds her hands in front of her on the table and leans forward.

"How are things going with Dana?" she asks.

My eyebrows shoot up. "Why?"

"Well," Mum says, "she seems like a nice girl. And you've been seeing her for a few months. Is it serious?"

"Does it matter? I graduate next year and then—" I pause.

"And then?" Dad prompts.

"I suppose I'll go to college. We'll break up then, if we're still together . . . I don't understand why you're asking me this."

Mum sighs.

"Ben, we're worried about you," Dad says.

Here we go.

"What is there to be worried about?" I have a feeling I know what's coming.

Mum looks at Dad like this is some big secret or something. Or maybe because she's thinking he has the same problem.

"Ben, it seems like you're having a tough summer," she says. "A tough year since—since your sister died." There's a pause. "We know about the drinking."

"The drinking," I repeat. I look at Dad. He's not saying anything. He's letting Mum do all the dirty work.

"Yes, and we're worried that you're driving, too, after. Have you done that?"

I want to lie. I want to tell her that I'd never be so stupid, not after they lost one child. I would hate for them to lose me, too, for something as irresponsible as driving drunk.

I can't lie to her, so I don't answer.

"Ben?" Dad says. "Mum asked you a question."

"Well, I usually stay at Guthrie's," I say. It's the truth. I usually do.

"That's your answer?" Dad says.

"What about the times you don't stay at Guthrie's?" Mum asks. "Sweetheart, you're not in trouble—we just want the truth. We want to help you. You need to make better decisions."

"Maybe once or twice." I take a drink of my Coke and wish I had some whiskey for it. I wave my hand toward Dad's glass. "You planning on driving after that beer?"

"Don't get smart with me," Dad says. "This is about you and your underage drinking."

"Tom," Mum says, and puts her hand on his arm. "We all need to find ways to deal with this, Ben. Some days are better than others. Some days I feel like I can't even get out of bed, I miss her so much. And I'm glad you have Guthrie and your fishing to help you. But I think you've made some poor choices."

"Fine. I won't drink and drive." I don't tell them I won't drink, though, and I hope that's enough. I want this to end.

Mum sighs and gives Dad that look again.

"There's something else," Dad says.

Our server sets down our plates, and I'm glad for the break in this pointless conversation. What else could they possibly have to say to me? I'm not going to stop drinking because they're worried about me. And I can't believe that hypocrite sitting across from me.

"Well?" I ask. No sense in prolonging this. I pick up one of the ribs, covered in thick homemade barbecue sauce.

"Ben, we want to talk to you about Lulu," Mum says.

I drop the rib, my appetite gone in an instant. "What?"

Mum takes a sip from her water goblet and then dabs at the corners of her mouth with her napkin. "Ben, did something happen between you two? Did you get into some sort of argument after Trixie died?"

"What?" I say again.

"She doesn't come to the house anymore. She barely says two words to us anytime she sees us. Today I saw her and Emily leaving the library, and when I waved at them, she pretended not to see me."

Dad jumps in. "And I've seen how the two of you are at the resort. You can barely stand to be in the same room."

"What happened?" Mum reaches across the table for my hand, and her tone is so gentle, so concerned, that it almost breaks me.

"Nothing happened." This is one of those moments that calls for anything but the truth. "She was Trixie's friend, not mine."

They don't need to know what I did, what I said.

Dad clears his throat. "But we see that things—like your

drinking—have gotten worse since school ended and you've—you've been around Lucy more."

I suck in a breath.

"And then—after Lucy went missing—" Mum starts, but I cut her off.

"She didn't go *missing*. She went to South Dakota. Big difference." I don't know why I say it.

"You've been so angry all summer, Ben," Mum says in her soothing voice. "And with Trixie's anniversary coming up—" Her voice breaks into a sob. "We miss Lulu, too, Ben, and we can't help but wonder if something happened between the two of you that has—well, has kept her away from us. We'd love to see her again."

Shit.

It's all I can do not to get up and walk away. I could do it. It's only five or six miles to Guthrie's house.

But it's Mum's birthday. I won't. Not today.

I've got to figure out a way to get them to stop talking. I couldn't lie to her about the drinking, but I lied to her when I said nothing happened between Lucy and me. I can lie to her again.

"I'll talk to her." The lie slips out, and it's surprisingly easy to keep going with it. "Don't worry, I'll take care of it, whatever it is."

Mum looks at me for a long time and tears pool in her eyes. She knows I'm lying. "Promise me, Ben. She lost her best friend."

Fuckall, she can't ask me to promise.

"Why are you so worried about Lucy?" I can't mask my anger. "So we're not friends anymore. Let it go!"

"Oh, sweetheart." Now the tears slip down her cheeks. "What if it had been Lucy instead of Trixie? How would Trixie have felt?"

Now I do it. I push away from the table. I don't want to listen to this anymore.

"Ben." Dad's voice is low, quiet. "Don't."

I take a deep breath. I won't. I won't do this to Mum on her birthday, at the Twenty-Seven Club, where we've had so many good times as a family. I sit back down.

"I'm sorry, Mum." I look down at my plate of food.

"And the drinking?" Mum says. "Please. I don't know what I'll do if something happens to you, too."

I nod. It's the best I can do. I'm all out of promises.

38 · Lucy

I WAKE IN THE NIGHT TO LOUD CRACKS OF THUNDER AND THE telephone ringing.

I sit up, my heart pounding. No one calls us on the landline except my grandparents.

Something is very wrong.

Oh, no, please. What if something's happened to one of my grandparents? Or Daniel?

By the time I make it downstairs, Mom's standing in the kitchen in her fuzzy peach-colored robe, her hand over her mouth, her eyes wide with shock or terror or pain, I don't know which.

"Oh, God, no," she says into the phone.

My dad is standing by the back door, pulling a long-sleeved denim shirt on over his white T-shirt. His face is pale, stubble lining his cheeks and chin. His brows furrow together.

"Get dressed, Luce," he says.

"What's happening?"

"Oh, God," Mom says again. "We're on our way."

She hangs up the phone. "There's a fire. The restaurant is on fire. I'll get dressed and we'll go."

She's amazingly calm, but her gray face and wide eyes give her away, flashing from one object in the room to another as though she's not sure where to focus.

I race upstairs but don't change out of my pajamas. I throw

a Twins hoodie on over my T-shirt and yoga pants and slip into a pair of flip-flops. I'm back downstairs in less than a minute.

Mom's right behind me; Dad's already waiting with the car running. Flashes of lightning fill the night sky, but it's not raining.

Why isn't it raining?

This cannot be happening.

The Full Loon cannot burn down.

We get to town just after midnight. Dad can't drive any farther than Sweet Pea's. The block is cordoned off, the flashing lights of police cars and fire trucks cutting across the darkness, an ethereal orange glow stretching into the black sky.

A crowd has gathered on both sides of the block. Mom gets out of the car before it's come to a full stop and pushes her way through the crowd toward the Full Loon. Dad and I follow her until a Crow Wing County sheriff's deputy stops her.

"That's my restaurant," she says. "Please."

The deputy must know her. He takes her arm and says, "Ginger, there's nothing you can do. Let the firefighters work."

"How bad? How bad is it?" Now that she's here, now that she sees the great orange flames leaping into the night sky, she's beginning to crack. I can hear it in her voice.

"Well, now," the sheriff's deputy says slowly, "they've done a good job of containing the fire. It hasn't spread to any other buildings, and that's a good thing, wouldn't you say?"

"What happened? How did it start?"

"Can't say for sure. Nature's giving us quite a lightning

show tonight, so that's a possibility. Or maybe it started in the kitchen, or from some faulty wiring. You never know."

"Bill," my mother says in her firm tone, "there is no faulty wiring at the Full Loon."

"I didn't mean to insult you or your fine establishment," Bill says. He turns to Dad and me. "Hey there, Cal."

Dad nods at him, then takes Mom by the arm. "Come on," he says. "We can see better from across the street."

I follow them. They stand on the sidewalk in front of the auto parts shop and huddle together, Dad's arm around Mom. A tear, watery orange with the reflection of the flames, slips down her cheek. I squeeze her hand, and she grips mine tightly. She doesn't let go for a long time, not until Daniel arrives and pulls her into a hug.

"Sis," he says, "don't you worry. We'll bounce back from this."

We stand and watch our family restaurant burn.

Eventually, the crowd thins. The fire chief and county sheriff talk to Mom and Dad and Daniel against the backdrop of thick, gray smoke. I'm so tired. I want to go home.

"Dad?" I reach out to touch his sleeve.

His eyes are gentle when he turns to look at me. "Oh, Luce. You must be exhausted. Do you think you can call Hannah to come get you? We're not going anywhere anytime soon."

I nod and send a text. *There's a fire at the café. I'm in town. Come get me?*

Even though it's nearly three in the morning, she does. Before I go, my mom hugs me tight, kisses the top of my head.

"Come home in the morning, okay?" she says. "Everything will be all right, I promise. We'll get through this."

My heart stutters as I remember the last time she said words like these—the day Trixie died.

But it wasn't. Everything was not all right.

I stand under the hot water of Hannah's shower for a long time, but no matter how many times I scrub my hair with her rosemary mint shampoo, the smoke has burrowed into every cell, every pore. I cannot wash it away.

Trixie's Heart

Trixie grew up to become a lovely young lady. She had a beautiful heart, good and pure and generous. She cared and loved and hurt when others were in pain. She took in all that concern for others and stored it safely in her heart. Her heart got bigger and fuller, and the bigger it got, the more she loved.

One summer day, Trixie went to the lake with three of the people who she loved the most: her brother, Ben, her best friend, Lulu, and Lulu's brother, Clay. It was a beautiful day with endless sunshine and a perfect blue sky. Bluebird skies, her brother would say. The four of them swam and laughed and relaxed in the sun.

Trixie looked at the three people who she loved so much lying in the sunshine and she made a wish. She wished that they would never know heartache. She wished that they would never know pain. She wished she could collect all their cares and worries and keep them close to her, in her own heart.

And so she did. She closed her eyes and willed all their sorrows and fears from their hearts to her own. Her heart was heavy and she staggered from the weight of it, but she was filled with happiness that she could do something so wonderful for the people she loved.

Then she had another idea. She would swim to the little island offshore, empty her heart of all the sadness and worry, and return lighthearted once more. She would be ready to collect the sorrows of everyone she knew, and they would know nothing but peace and joy.

She slipped into the lake and swam toward the island. As she glided through the cool water, she felt light and free, even though her heart strained against the weight of worry and sadness. Before she could reach the island, her beautiful, fragile heart could no longer bear the extra burden. Her heart split in two and then shattered, and from the wreckage, the sorrows and cares of her beloved friends returned to them twofold.

For not only were they now once again weighed down with the sadness of everyday life, they were doubly burdened by the loss of their dear Trixie.

Without her, the three people she loved the most—Ben, Lulu, and Clay—drifted away from one another, to carry alone their sorrows and the remaining shards of Trixie's broken heart.

AUGUST

Being deeply loved by someone gives you strength,
while loving someone deeply gives you courage.
—*Lao Tzu*

39 · Ben

THE FIRST WEEK OF AUGUST IS A SLOW ONE AT THE RESORT. Every year the same family rents every cabin for a family reunion, three sisters in their sixties and their kids and grandkids. Nobody wants to fish, or if they do, they get a small container of night crawlers and cast off the dock. So I've got a couple of extra days off. Guthrie and I take the pontoon out and fish for walleye. It's Monday, but we won't be having the usual at the Full Loon tonight, not since the fire last week. When I ran into Daniel at the bait shop, he said it would be a couple more weeks before they open.

"So you know Hannah Mills?" Guthrie asks. He flips his shades onto the top of his head. "Lucy's friend?"

Lucy's friend. Of course I know Hannah Mills. Everyone knows Hannah Mills.

"Yeah. What about her?"

"I'm taking her out this week."

"Taking her out? Like on a date?" I can't remember the last time Guthrie asked a girl out on a date—tenth grade, maybe?

"Well, what else?"

"Hannah Mills?"

"Yes. Hannah Mills."

"I don't get it. Why would you go on a date with her?"

"Why are you dating Dana?"

"This isn't about me, and it sure as hell isn't about Dana. When did you decide you like Hannah Mills? And isn't she going out with that stupid cowboy?"

"They broke up right after the rodeo."

I grit my teeth. I don't like to think about the rodeo. "You haven't answered my question."

"I ran into Hannah at Sweet Pea's last week."

Sweet Pea's. I think about the fudge that Lucy gave to Emily, the same kind she used to bring to me.

"Why were you at the candy store?" There's a tug on my line but it goes slack again.

"I wasn't. I was at the Broken Spine and I saw Hannah at Sweet Pea's. So I went in to say hi."

"And?"

"I like Hannah. She smiles a lot. She's funny. And she's hot. The best part, though? She lets me talk."

"So was Lucy with her?" I ask.

Guthrie sighs. "Lucy's grounded. You know that."

"Never mind. That's great about you and Hannah. I hope it works out for you."

Guthrie shakes his head but doesn't say anything else.

He doesn't have to.

There's another tug on my line, and this time, it holds. I lift the tip of my rod and gently reel him in, a crappie. He goes into the net without a fight. I take the hook out and drop the fish into the live well.

Guthrie laughs. "You keeping that?"

"Yeah." I dig into the container of leeches. "You catch any

sunnies or crappies, throw them in here, okay? I'll take them home for Mum."

It's been a long time since we had a fish fry. I can almost taste the sweet, batter-fried fillets.

"I'm officially inviting myself over for dinner." Guthrie pulls up a good-size bluegill. "Well, what do we have here? Looks like this is our lucky day."

We fill the live well with sunfish and crappies and a couple of walleye and head back to Guthrie's to clean them. I'm not a fan of this part, but Guthrie is quick and skilled with the fillet knife. I clean up the mess while he packs the fillets in ice, and then we head over to my house.

The house is empty and dark, the blinds closed up tight. There's a note from Mum on the counter: *Upstairs with a migraine. There's leftover roast in the refrigerator. Love you.*

I hand the note to Guthrie. "Looks like our fish fry will have to wait."

He looks at the paper for a moment. "They'll keep."

"Yeah, let's get them in the freezer." I pull open a drawer for the roll of aluminum foil.

"You okay?"

I look up, surprised. "What?"

"Are you okay?"

I shrug. "Yeah. It's just fish, you know?"

He takes the box of aluminum foil, tears off a sheet, and begins wrapping packets of fillets. "Yeah, they'll keep," he says again, quietly, almost to himself.

40 · Lucy

Summer unravels.

August has arrived, and with it the fact that soon it will be one year.

I am moving forward. Trixie is not.

Trixie is now memories and stories and photographs in frames and albums and scrapbooks. The *Trixies* I tell to a little girl who misses a cousin she barely knew.

I'm still grounded. The fire at the restaurant caused a lot of damage to the kitchen and part of the back dining room. They say it was the lightning that night after all. The timing couldn't have been worse, in the middle of the summer tourist season, but they're hoping to reopen in a couple of weeks.

At least Mom is talking to me again since the fire. I guess she must have decided that, in the grand scheme of things, my refusal to work that Monday night shift isn't such a big deal.

Simon has come over twice. I'm worried, though, that someone will come home and find him here, and I can't do that to my parents. Not now, after South Dakota and the fire.

So I tell him he needs to go; he kisses me. He sends me text messages; he misses me.

Today, he and Shay are taking a day trip up to Lake Itasca, the headwaters of the Mississippi River, an hour and a half away. I watch them drive off from the kitchen window.

It strikes me that I won't miss him when he's gone—not today, not after he goes back to St. Paul.

I run upstairs to my room for my phone and call Hannah, who picks up right away.

"I should miss him, right?" My breathing is heavy.

"Lucille? Miss who? Is everything okay?"

"Simon. I should miss him, right, when he's not around? Isn't that how love works? You want to be with a person all the time, and when you can't, it's like a piece of you is missing?"

She doesn't answer right away.

"Hannah?"

"You miss Ben."

I don't need to say anything. I've never stopped missing Ben.

"I think you know what you need to do. I really had high hopes for Simon, though." She sighs. "I wish I could come over."

"Me, too. I miss you."

Hannah laughs. "That's how you know it's love. I love you, too, Lucille."

I end the call and lean my head against the wall. The next time Simon sneaks over, I'll tell him that it's not working, that we should break up.

I take a deep breath. I don't want to think about this anymore. I grab a book and walk down to the patio to take advantage of the fact that Shay's not using it today.

But the words are a jumble on the page. My mind wanders.

It's too quiet.

I'm too alone.

I find my iPod and slip my earbuds in and walk into town, cutting through Sullivan Street Park.

I walk the trail and sit at the edge of the lake, my toes in the sand. I close my eyes and count the days until summer ends.

My phone buzzes with a text—a photo of Simon standing next to the tall marker at the headwaters, then another of him standing in shallow Lake Itasca. *Missing u @ the Mississippi. Wish u were here.*

I don't respond.

I stand up, brush the sand off my shorts, and cut through the woods on the path that leads to the back parking lot of the Gas-n-Go. I'm inside the convenience store reaching for a bottle of water in the cooler when I hear my name. I turn to see Daniel.

Of course.

"Whatcha doing here, Lucy?" he asks me. "Aren't you grounded?"

I hold up the water. "It's a long walk home. Would you rather I succumb to dehydration and heat exhaustion?"

"Shouldn't you already be at home?"

"Daniel, come on. I couldn't take it anymore. I needed fresh air. Exercise."

"I'll give you a ride home. I'm on my way to Brainerd anyway."

He fills me in on the day's progress at the Full Loon. "It's going to be better than ever. We're coming back strong, Luce."

When I don't respond, he says, "I haven't seen you

much since you got back from South Dakota. Everything okay?"

"Well, no. I got *grounded*, remember? For life?"

"Never been grounded before, huh?"

I shake my head. "No, and they threw the book at me, didn't they?"

Daniel laughs. "Everybody was pretty worried about you, Lucy. I can't blame them for being so upset."

"The worst is that I can't see Hannah. Guthrie is throwing her a birthday party, and Mom and Dad won't let me go."

"Well, the way I see it, and shit if I'm not going to sound just like my dad, and probably yours, you have to accept the consequences of your actions. And if that means not seeing Hannah and missing her birthday, there it is."

I swipe at a tear in the corner of my eye. "It's not fair. Clayton can get away with murder. I make one mistake—one— and I'm punished for weeks! I *need* to see Hannah."

Suddenly I get an idea. Daniel can help me get to that party.

"Daniel," I say, leaning toward him. "You've got to convince Mom to let me go to the party."

"Oh, no," he says. "No way. I'm not getting in the middle of this."

"Please, I'm begging you. This summer has been awful. *Please.*"

He's quiet for a long time. Then: "I can't make any prom- ises, but I'll do what I can. Don't fuck this up, okay?"

"Okay, yes, thank you." The words rush out of me.

"Seriously, don't mess this up."

As if this summer could get any more messed up.

By the time Mom gets home, I've showered again and made tacos for dinner. She comes out to the deck, where I'm sitting with my laptop, pinning quotes to my online bulletin board.

I don't regret the things I've done. I only regret the things I didn't do when I had the chance.

I can picture that quote in our notebook, one of Trixie's favorites, written in dark teal cursive.

Don't count the laps—make the laps count. Trixie's favorite swim team quote.

I would rather walk with a friend in the dark, than alone in the light. One of the many Helen Keller quotes I wrote in the book.

I close the laptop when I hear the sliding door open.

"Hey, Luce." Mom flops down into the chair next to me. "What an exhausting day. But the new roof is on, so that's a relief, at least. And the painters come tomorrow."

"Mm-hmm," I say. Daniel already told me. "That's great."

"Dinner smells fantastic."

"Dad's not home yet. I figured tacos would be easy enough to reheat."

"Good thinking. I'm exhausted," she says again. "So what have you been up to today?"

"Oh, you know," I say, "the usual. A load of laundry, a little reading."

"What were you doing just now?"

"Do you remember that notebook Trixie and I used to keep? Quotes and song lyrics and stuff like that?"

She smiles. "The Book of Quotes?"

I nod. "Well, I started a new online board with some of the quotes. The ones I can remember, anyway."

"Don't you have the notebook?"

I shake my head. "No. It's at Trixie's."

She frowns. "You haven't asked for it?"

"No."

"Honey, it's important to you. I'm sure Jane and Tom would understand if you—"

I cut her off. "No, it's okay. Plus, I don't really see them, you know?"

"I'll call Jane right now." Mom stands up.

I reach out and grab her arm to stop her. "No, please don't. It's not important, Mom. Don't bother them."

She looks at me for a minute, then says softly, "Maybe you could ask Ben to find it for you, then."

I pinch my lips together and shake my head again.

Mom smiles. "Hey, I just had a great idea. We're painting some sections of the walls at the restaurant with blackboard paint. Why don't you pick out a few of your favorite quotes, and you and Hannah can write them on the walls with chalk? It would be a nice way to honor Trixie's memory."

I pick up my laptop and nod. Since the fire, Mom hasn't been as angry with me, but I know that her disappointment is still there, simmering beneath the surface. I don't want to disappoint her again. "Yeah, I can do that."

"Lucy? Think about asking Ben for the notebook, okay?"

That I can't do.

41 · Ben

I'VE BEEN WASTED SINCE YESTERDAY. I FIGURE I DON'T HAVE to work for a couple of days, so why not? After Guthrie and I wrapped all that fish and packed it into the freezer, I found the key to the liquor cabinet on the counter next to an empty lowball glass. Like it was waiting for me. Convenient.

Wasted is good, helps me forget.

Wasted means I can't hear Mum crying in Trixie's room as we get closer to the anniversary.

Dad isn't drunk, but he's drinking. He and Mum don't notice that I'm drunk; they don't notice me at all.

I send a text to Guthrie: *Dude, you gotta come get me. Can't drive too wasted but I gotta get outta here.*

I've been able to keep that promise to Mum at least. I slam the front door shut behind me, but I don't know that either of my parents will hear it or care. My phone sounds with the ringtone Dana picked out for herself. I ignore it. I don't want to see her.

God, I'm in a pissy mood.

Guthrie pulls up in his shitty Impala. Hannah Mills is with him, his girlfriend. The new girl. Lucy's new best friend. The girl who took Trixie's place. On the drive to Guthrie's, I try to work it out in my head—how it's possible that this cowgirl and my Lulu are friends.

Slumped in the backseat, I laugh. I laugh and I can't stop.

She's not my Lulu. Not Lulu. I'm so confused. She bought me fudge again. I know that fudge she gave Emily was really for me. I know it. But she didn't give it to me. Why didn't she give it to me? Because I'm an asshole, that's why.

Shit, I'm messed up.

Hannah turns around and gives me this look, like she thinks I've lost it and maybe I have. But then she smiles at me—she understands, she gets it. I see it in her eyes and her smile. She's a sweet girl. No wonder Guthrie likes her. No wonder she's Lucy's best friend. She reaches over and squeezes my hand and then turns back.

It's raining again. No fire tonight. We sit in Guthrie's basement and watch *The Outlaw Josey Wales*. Or they do. Or maybe they don't. They whisper to each other, laugh, sit close together on the couch. I drink another beer and wonder what it would be like to be with Lucy like that. We never got our chance.

At some point the movie ends, and Guthrie peels himself away from Hannah and goes upstairs. She turns to me.

"Ben," she says, "you okay?"

I nod.

"You want to ask me anything?" she says.

Shit. I mean, I know I'm fucked up, but what the fuck is this girl talking about?

"What the fuck are you talking about?" I ask.

She laughs, her head thrown back. "Well, you sure got a brick in your hat tonight, don't ya?"

Guthrie finally found the perfect girl. They both talk shit.

"A brick in my hat?"

"Means drunk," Guthrie says from upstairs.

She leans toward me and says in a low voice, "You want to ask me about Lucy, don't you? You want to know if she really likes Simon or if she's still carrying a torch for you, right?" She smiles, big and toothy, and flips her hair over her shoulder.

Ah, so that's what this is all about. Lucy.

"Carrying a torch for me? You've got to be kidding me. That torch went out a long time ago."

She shakes her head. "I don't think so."

"Lucy and I aren't friends anymore," I say, and it feels strange, wrong. Like putting it in a simple sentence takes the truth out of it.

"So I hear."

"Have you seen her?"

She shakes her head again. "Still grounded."

"Have you talked to her?" Why am I doing this? Why am I putting myself through this?

"Yeah. I miss her."

I take a swig of beer. *Me, too,* I think, and then I think I might have said it out loud. The words echo, bounce around in my head.

"You want to know what I think, Ben?" Hannah finally says, frowning. "I haven't even known Lucy for a year, but she's the most loyal person I've ever met and she loves like crazy. She'd do anything for someone she loves."

I'm with her so far.

"Even if it's someone who's a complete asshole to her and

says awful things. You've gotta stop hurting her." The air leaves my lungs, deflates me. "Just stop."

She knows. Hannah knows.

Guthrie comes back downstairs with a pizza. He offers me a slice, but I wave him away.

I have no appetite. I sit here and drink beer and when I close my eyes, I see Lucy, loyal and loving like crazy. I see her, us, like we're in a movie, sitting in my Firebird and it's raining and I lean over and turn her face toward me and I kiss her. I kiss her like I mean it.

That kiss, it meant something.

Hannah's right. I've been a complete asshole. I said awful things.

But how could she still love me, be loyal to me, after how I've treated her?

How will she ever forgive me?

42 · *Lucy*

DANIEL HELPED ME GET TO HANNAH'S PARTY, AND NOW I WISH I'd stayed home.

Story Lake Road is narrow and twisty, about fifteen miles west of town off County Road 27. The road hugs the edge of Story Lake on one side and Papyrus Lake on the other. The Guthries live out at the end at the channel, where the lakes meet, in a gorgeous Victorian-style home that looks like something out of a film. The huge backyard slopes down to a rocky beach that's packed with people from school.

Simon is clingy. He reaches for my hand, puts an arm around my waist.

This is the first time we've seen each other in days.

Hannah thinks I should break up with him tonight. "It ain't a party till something gets broke," she said.

"I've missed you." Simon kisses my forehead. "What do you want to drink?"

Before I can answer, Hannah calls out, "Lucille, do one more shot with me. Please? Pretty please? For my birthday?"

I shrug at Simon and follow Hannah to the kitchen. The amber liquor bites and cuts, like swallowing hot glass. I gasp and she hands me another glass, something purple and sweet that cools the fire. She squeezes my hand. She's grinning and off-kilter.

"Darlin'," she says, her twang intensified by the booze, "I love you so much. So much. You are the world's greatest friend, Lucy

Lucille, and don't you ever forget it. You are special. And don't let anyone—not a single one of these assholes here—tell you any different."

She hugs me and then squeals when Guthrie walks into the kitchen. "Isn't he the cutest?" she whispers. She grabs his hand, winks at me, and leads him out to the deck.

I find an empty corner in the living room and curl up on a wide armchair with thick, soft cushions. I close my eyes and try to block out the noise of the karaoke from downstairs. I imagine that I'm somewhere else, the sunroom at Trixie's house or down by the lake, on the beach. In my mind, in the best stretches of my imagination, this summer has not happened. There was no South Dakota. No Simon.

But I know that you can't wish an entire summer away. I've tried.

My mind in its haze shifts. Last August. Hot and humid. I'd stayed at Trixie's house the night before. When I woke up, Jane was in the kitchen with fresh scones and English breakfast tea. She and I ate in the sunroom and waited for Trixie and Ben to wake up. When Trixie joined us she was dressed in her swimsuit, a pair of Halcyon Lake track shorts, and flip-flops. Her hair sat in a high bun on the top of her head. Ben, though, came down in his pajamas—an old camo Cabela's T-shirt with a frayed hem and plaid sleep pants. His curly hair stood out in every direction and he smiled when he saw me. A beautiful, content smile that hinted at something else. Something more.

"You going to the beach today?" he asked Trixie. He sat down next to her and reached over her plate for a scone.

She nodded. "Sullivan Street. Gonna go early and snag the swim raft."

"Maybe I'll text Clayton and we'll come, too."

"Whatever," Trixie said, and poured a cup of tea.

Jane patted Trixie's hand. And I'll never forget what she said.

"I'm the luckiest mum on the planet, you know, that the two of you get along so well."

"Eh," Ben said, his mouth full.

"Whatever," Trixie said again.

Ben swallowed. "Mum, she's barely tolerable and you know it." He grinned. I could see a tiny blueberry lodged in one of his top teeth.

I smiled at Ben, and when I glanced at Trixie, she winked at me.

At that moment, I could never have imagined this—my life now. In Guthrie's living room, avoiding the crowd in the basement, where Hannah is belting out a lopsided version of "Stand by Your Man." Ben and his girlfriend are here somewhere. Ben, who kissed me, once. And Simon, how could I possibly forget about Simon, my boyfriend? Where is Simon? I need to tell him that I'm actually in love with Ben.

No, no. I can't do that. I am getting over him. I am getting over Ben. Right? But I still miss him.

Fuzzy. The world is fuzzy. I stand up, sway, put my palm on the wall to steady myself. I will find Hannah and tell her we need to go. Or I need to. She should stay—it's her birthday, after all. I shake my head. Neither one of us can drive.

I'm stuck.

I've been stuck all summer.

I make my way down the stairs to the basement, gripping the handrail along the stairs so tightly my knuckles turn white.

The basement is dark. A spinning disco ball flashes purple-and-silver light onto the walls, the carpet, the couches. Guthrie stands at the front of the room destroying a Garth Brooks song. Dana untangles herself from Ben's arms and walks past me with a pitying look. I don't want her pity. I close my eyes so I don't have to see her. If I can't see her, she can't see me. If I can't see Ben, Ben can't see me.

"Where's your boyfriend?" A low growl from the couch.

Ben can see me. I have been able to avoid him since we got here, but I cannot avoid the truth of *us*. Of me, loving him. My stomach flips, and I teeter a little as I step over his legs, which are stretched out in front of him.

I want him to reach out, pull me onto his lap, kiss me like he did in the Firebird, until I forget who I am, forget everything.

"Lucille!" Hannah cries. "It's about damn time! Where have you *been*?"

I take another step but Ben sticks his leg out in front of me and I stumble. Once I right myself, I turn to glare at him.

"What do you think you're doing?" I hiss.

"I asked you a question," Ben says. His eyes are glassy but he sounds normal, calm. "Where's your boyfriend?"

"Mind your own business, Ben," Hannah says, and pulls me closer. "Now's not the time for this."

"It *is* my business," Ben says.

"Since when?" I ask, my voice trembling. *Why* is he talking to me?

"Since always," Ben says.

Oh.

"Ben," Hannah says, and makes a deliberate, overstated move to face him, "*where* has Dana gone?"

"Yeah." I stick out my chin. "You might not get laid tonight if she sees you talking to me."

"Be careful, Lucy," Ben says.

"Who the hell do you think you are?" I say, but then I furrow my brow. I'm not sure that the words have come out right.

I look at him, at his lips, at his eyes, dark with anger and a need that reflects my own. I need Ben. I do.

"Ignore him," Hannah says, and she pulls me down on the couch next to her in time to hear Guthrie's big finish. Hannah claps and whistles.

"Your turn," Guthrie says to Hannah, and when she stands, he pulls her close and kisses her.

"Come on, hon," she says to me, and even in my hazy state I know that there is no way I can get out of this. "I know what you like."

And then, before I really know what's happening, I hear Blondie's "The Tide Is High" coming from the small, tinny speakers.

We sing and dance, and for a minute or two I forget that Ben is there. Then Dana comes back down the stairs and hands Ben a beer. When I look up again, Simon is standing next to the karaoke machine, scrolling through the display. Hannah and I bow to Guthrie's weak applause. She bounds over to the couch, scoots onto Guthrie's lap, and kisses him. I have to look away.

"Hey," Simon says, "sing with me." He pulls me close, his arms around my waist.

"Where've you been?" I ask.

He smiles. "Down by the lake. And the fire pit. This place is amazing."

"You've been here before," I snap. "What's so amazing about it this time?"

He drops his arms away from me. "What's the matter? Did I do something wrong?"

Yes. He did something wrong. He's been nice to me all summer; he's tried to love me and that's his big mistake.

I shake my head.

"Lucy, are you drunk?" He moves his hands back to my waist, pulls me close.

I snort. "Well, yes, aren't you?"

He nuzzles my neck, and I can smell tequila on his breath. My stomach lurches. "Sing with me," he murmurs.

"I don't sing karaoke."

"Really? What were you doing just now? Singing karaoke, right, with Hannah?"

"Yes, but, um, my catalog is pretty limited."

He pulls back and looks at me, a half smile playing on his lips like he's not sure if he should laugh or be angry. "Your catalog is limited," he repeats.

"That's what I said."

"How limited? Or is it that you don't want to sing with me?" He looks hurt.

I'm tired and drunk and I don't want to fight with Simon, because isn't that where this is going? I don't want to fight with Simon in front of Ben.

Ben must want to fight with Simon though, because he stands up and steps in between us, his face close to Simon's. How did he hear us?

"She sings three songs, dickwad. Three."

My insides flip. Ben remembers.

Simon gives Ben a small push, then steps back when Ben doesn't move. "Oh, yeah?" Simon's voice cracks a little. "What three?"

Like it matters.

"Blondie, 'The Tide Is High.' Prince, 'I Would Die 4 U.' Britney Spears, '. . . Baby One More Time.'" Ben ticks them off on his fingers.

"Come on, Ben," Dana says. When did Dana come back? She's standing next to Ben, her hand on his arm.

"How the hell would you know?" Simon says. He turns toward me. "Why do you keep letting this guy mess with you, Lucy? You deserve someone much better."

Now Ben pushes Simon, who staggers back toward the wall. "I suppose you think you're that someone?"

Hannah bounces up from the couch and laughs, puts herself right in between them. "Ben, that sounds like a line from a bad movie. Now why don't you move along and leave this poor boy alone? Go on."

Her accent is extra SoDak tonight. She's laying it on thick.

"Dana, sweetie?" she says. "Why don't you take Ben on out of here?"

I think I'm going to throw up. Too much booze, too much Simon, too much Ben. Not enough Ben. Never enough Ben.

I need air. My cheeks are damp. When did I start crying?

God, why can't I stop crying?

I push past Simon and Hannah and Ben and Dana, up the stairs, out to the backyard where I kneel in the dirt in front of a honeysuckle bush and throw up. The dense scent of the blossoms mixes with the sickening sour-sweetness of too much booze coming back up. It settles into my nose and burns the back of my throat. I retch over and over until my stomach hurts and finally the tears stop.

I'm alone in Guthrie's yard, I've puked my guts out, Trixie is dead, and no matter what I do, I'm still in love with Ben Porter.

I walk down to the beach. All along the edge of the woods, there are stacks of rocks, just like at Lake Superior, the ones that Ben called inuksuit.

He is everywhere I go.

I hear shouting, yelling, someone calling my name. I think it's Simon, but there's another voice, too, this one louder. I hear the crack, bone on bone, more shouting. I look up toward Guthrie's house and there are two shapes near the patio, hitting each other. I should stop them. It might be Ben.

Instead, I lie down and reach out to touch the cool rocks.

43 · Ben

S<small>IMON FOLLOWS ME OUTSIDE TO THE PATIO AND HE SAYS THIS:</small>

"Lucy doesn't love you. She loves me. I can prove it. We—we slept together in South Dakota."

He's lying, I know it. I know Lucy. Or maybe I don't. Either way, I beat the shit out of that useless douchebag, which is easy enough because he's totally blotto. The crack of my fist against his face is satisfying, so much that I do it again and again, until Eddie pulls me off him.

Finally Simon staggers away from me, blood streaming from his nose.

I find Lucy down by the lake, lying in the sand. I go to her. I pick her up, and it's like she weighs nothing—she is empty. She smells like rum and vomit, her hair is wild, her face streaked with tears and dirt. She is beautiful, my Lulu.

I carry her to the screen porch and sit down on an old sofa with her head in my lap. I close my eyes and stroke her hair and listen to her breathe.

That's how Dana finds us.

"Ben?"

My eyes snap open. Dana stands in front of me, one hand covering her mouth, her eyes wide. Oh, shit.

"It's all true, isn't it?" she says.

I untangle my fingers from Lucy's hair. "What's true?"

"You—you and Lucy Meadows. Have you been *cheating* on me with Lucy Meadows?" Her voice cracks.

"No." That's it, one word.

"Then what is *this*?" Dana cries.

"This is me taking care of a friend." I want it to be true.

"But—but you and *Lucy* are *not* friends!"

"We used to be friends," I say. "She needs someone to take care of her, and I happened to be around."

"Taking care of Lulu Meadows when she's *drunk* is not *your* job, Ben."

I suck in a breath. Did she just call Lucy *Lulu*? She couldn't have, she couldn't have known that's what we called her.

"Where's her boyfriend? Don't you think he should be the one taking care of her?"

I have never seen Dana so upset, and the fact that she's upset because of me, because of something I've done, isn't lost on me.

"I don't know where Simon is," I tell her. "My guess is that he left after I beat the shit out of him."

She gasps. "*You* did that? You beat up Lucy's boyfriend, and then I find you out here with her? Ben, what is going on with you?"

What is going on with me is something that should have gone on a long time ago.

"Dana, I think we should break up."

She lets out a long exhale.

I'm expecting her to argue, but she doesn't say a word. I

can hardly stand to look at her as emotions cross her face—sadness, disappointment, and God, what is that? A tiny bit of relief? She takes a deep breath, but long moments pass before she finally speaks.

"Be kind to her, Ben. Take care of her. She deserves that."

God, she's being so nice about this, but I'm not surprised. She's always been the better person.

She turns and walks away.

"I'm sorry," I call to her, because it seems like the right thing to say, but I'm not. I don't feel sorry.

What I feel is heavy. A boulder of regret in my chest where my heart should be.

Lucy stirs on my lap, but she doesn't wake. I slip my fingers into her soft hair, massage her temple.

"Shh," I whisper. "I'll take care of you."

I've loved her all along.

44 · Lucy

THE DAY AFTER GUTHRIE'S PARTY, I CAN'T MOVE. MY BODY HAS rejected the horrible things I put inside it, and I deserve every bit of the nausea and achiness and throbbing headache. I don't remember how I got home, but it must have been Guthrie or Eddie—they were the only sober ones.

I guess Daniel will be disappointed, because I really messed this up.

"Was it worth it?" Dad asks as I walk past him. He's sitting in the recliner watching the Twins game. "You smell awful. And you don't look so good, either."

"Thanks," I mumble.

"I hope you're getting this whole rebellious teenager thing out of your system."

I would roll my eyes if I thought I could do it without throwing up. I stretch out on the sofa, and when the spinning stops, say, "You were the one who wanted me to make new friends and do stuff."

"What stuff did you do? Shots of tequila?"

That's possible. I'm not even sure.

He sighs. "So let me get this straight. You beg Daniel to talk us into letting you go to this party, which he does, and this is how you repay us? By getting wasted?"

I cringe. "I wouldn't say I begged, exactly."

"I don't even think we need to punish you for this," Dad

says and waves his hand in my direction. "I'm pretty sure you're feeling enough punishment right now."

He's got that right.

"I take it you're not going to the parade, then?" he asks.

Oh, the parade. Watermelon Days. I've never missed a Watermelon Days parade.

The last thing I need today, though, is the too-bright sunshine, the loud marching bands.

"I'm still grounded, remember?"

He doesn't answer. The game is back on, and I watch it, too, like I used to do when I was a kid. We'd get a pocket-size schedule at the gas station every April and mark the games we wanted to watch. Clay would fish with us, but he hated baseball. Watching the Twins was something special I did with my dad, just the two of us.

"Look," Dad says after the inning ends, "I talked to Mom and we think that maybe we've been too hard on you. We know this is a tough time for you, Lucy, and maybe we shouldn't have kept you away from your friends. So we're going to reduce your sentence."

"Really?" I cry. The sound of my own voice rattles inside my head. This is so backward. He should be adding to my sentence, not eliminating it. But I'll take it. "I'd hug you, but I don't think I should move."

"Don't screw this up again, Lucy. You've done some really stupid things. Knock it off, okay?"

"Okay," I say. "Thank you."

"I mean it."

"I know."

At a commercial break, Dad gets up and goes into the kitchen. He comes back a few minutes later with an ice pack, two small orange pills, a cup of coffee, and a banana.

"This should help," he says.

My phone buzzes as I swallow the painkillers—Hannah.

Holy shit what got into u last night?

Ha. Too much booze, that's what.

U know Ben beat Simon to a pulp right n then dumped Dana? Shits getn real babe.

My stomach drops, and I really am going to be sick. I didn't imagine it, Ben and Simon fighting.

Wait. Ben broke up with Dana?

I'm so tired, so confused, I can't think about it. Everything is so complicated.

Another buzz: *Luuuuuuceeeee r u there?*

I text back: *Funny story, Dad eased up on me. I'm not grounded anymore.*

In seconds: *I'm picking u up and we r going to that parade.*

Forty-five minutes later, Hannah knocks on the door and lets herself in. I haven't moved.

"Holy hell, Lucy, it's stifling in here. And it stinks. Oh, hi, Mr. Meadows." She grabs my arm, hauls me up, and pushes me toward the stairs. "You, my friend, need a shower."

I stand under the hot spray and let myself cry—everything that I do remember about last night rushes through my mind. Shots, karaoke, the beach. The replay stops there.

After I'm dressed, I grab my sunglasses from the top of my dresser. The treasure chest is there, Ben's agate nestled among the stones. I open the lid and roll it between my finger and thumb. I've missed the slight weight of it, the only solid, unbreakable thing in my life for so long. I slip it back into my pocket.

Hannah drives us into town to watch the parade in front of the Full Loon, which soft-opened Thursday night. We have to park a few blocks up the hill, and I'm glad that we're walking on the side of the street opposite Ben's house. Jane and Tom and Ben sit in lawn chairs at the edge of their yard. My heart pounds. There is an empty chair next to Ben.

Is it for Trixie? She loved Watermelon Days, especially the parade.

I'm socked with a memory. Watermelon Days, three years ago. Trixie and I were thirteen, the first year our parents let us go to the carnival on our own. The sun disappeared behind the trees; we had fistfuls of tickets for rides and games and mini-donuts. The night stretched before us, all twinkling, spinning lights and excitement.

"This is going to be a night we'll never forget," Trixie said, and squeezed my arm.

And she was right, but the night was memorable for a reason other than carnival rides and cotton candy. Trixie ditched me after a ride on the Ferris wheel.

"I need to use the satellite," she said. "I'll be right back."

Ten minutes passed and I walked over to the portable toilets to find her. There was a short line, but Trixie wasn't in it. I waited and watched as every door opened but she never emerged. I was certain that I'd missed her, that we'd passed each other and she'd be waiting back at the Ferris wheel.

She wasn't there.

I felt sick from the greasy food, the rides, the realization that Trixie had left me. She'd never done anything like that before. I sat on a bench and tried hard not to cry. But the tears fell anyway. I swiped at them but not fast enough when Clayton, Guthrie, and Ben found me.

Ben dropped down on the bench next to me. "What's up? Where's Trix?"

I shrugged. I was afraid to speak, afraid my words might break into sobs.

"Didn't we see her on the Fire Ball with that kid from metal shop, Kyle something?" Clayton asked. "Did she ditch you?"

I shrugged again. My best friend sneaked off to be with a boy. An older boy. Three years older, if he was in a class with Clayton. Why would she do that to me? It was so unlike her. We looked forward to the Watermelon Days carnival every year. We'd been talking about it for weeks, how excited we were that we could go off on our own now. I felt young and childish and left behind.

"No, it's nothing," I said to Clayton, but my voice wavered.

"It's not nothing," Ben said in a low voice, and he put his arm around me.

My heart soared in spite of the ache of Trixie's betrayal.

"You want me to call Dad to come get you?" Clayton asked.

Before I could answer, Ben stood and pulled me up, too, by

my elbow. "Nah, she's not going home. She's coming with us. Why waste all those tickets?"

He winked at me, and I let myself believe it was about more than the tickets.

I spent the rest of the night with them. Ben shared his deep-fried pickles and rode the spinning strawberries with me even though Clayton called me a baby. And when we finally met up with Trixie and Kyle from metal shop, holding hands in the line for the Zipper, I wasn't even mad anymore.

"Lulu," Trixie squealed on the walk home, "can you believe it? I ran into Kyle, and he asked me to ride the Fire Ball with him. I mean, how could I say no to that? You understand, right? And besides, you got to spend the night with Ben!"

I haven't thought of that night for a long time, how Trixie had left me, and Ben was there to pick up the pieces.

Hannah picks up the pieces now.

"Feel better?" she asks after we settle in, and she reaches her arm around me to hug me.

I nod. "Thanks."

"Babe, the best thing to do for a hangover is to keep moving."

"Where's Guthrie? Didn't you want to watch the parade with him?"

"He asked me, but I told him no, my girl needs me. We'll meet up at the carnival later."

"Tell me what happened last night."

She laughs. "Which part? The part where Ben pounded Simon or the part where Dana found you with your head on Ben's lap?"

My head on Ben's lap? A thought swims through my muddled brain, of Ben's fingers in my hair, but I don't know if it's memory or imagination.

"I guess I don't want to know after all," I murmur.

"Have you heard from him?"

"Ben?"

"Or Simon?"

I shake my head.

"Hon," she says. "You need to tell Simon it's over. I mean, he knows about you and Ben, right?"

"I would guess that the events of last evening probably erased any doubts he had about me and Ben, yes."

"Look, when the Renters showed up, I thought, *Perfect, this is exactly what she needs, a cute guy to get her mind off the jackass.* And Simon's so sweet to you, for a little while I thought it might actually work."

"Yeah," I said, "me, too. But Ben's everywhere I go, you know? I mean, look, I can't even watch a parade without him being right across the street."

"He's not right across the street, Luce. He's down the block. And it's not like you can avoid him in this town."

"I can try, can't I?"

"Let Simon down easy, okay?" Hannah says. "He's a nice guy, but you have to end it with him. Because, darlin', Ben is more than just across the street. He's in your heart."

The Day Lulu Made a New Friend

On Lulu's first first day of school without Trixie, her footsteps echoed in the empty hallways. The hour was early, too early, but she needed the quiet, the time before the rooms filled up and the teachers looked on her with pity in their sad eyes, for they, too, missed the happy girl called Trixie.

She found her locker and emptied the books and notebooks and pens from her backpack. She walked through the school, out a back door, to the long stretch of picnic tables and leafy trees that stood guard over the grand lake.

She had never felt as alone as she did at that moment, in this place where she and Trixie ate lunch on days when the sun warmed them and the scent of lilac and violet carried on the cool breeze.

Lulu took in a deep breath of the crisp, late summer air, now tinged with a sharp trace of algae bloom. She walked back into the school to spend that first day with the classmates she'd known her entire life, but who would never be the kind of friend to her that Trixie had been, since the very first first day of school.

She walked to her homeroom in the media center, where a girl sat alone at one of the tables, a girl Lulu didn't know. Her blond hair swirled around her like cotton candy.

Lulu was filled with a wave of courage.

Lulu smiled at the girl.

"Hi," she said. "I'm Lucy."

"My name's Hannah," the girl said. "Want to sit here?"

Lulu nodded, and when Hannah smiled at her, Lulu's heart lit up like a carnival ride.

45 · Ben

I get home from Guthrie's around noon and take a quick shower. The knuckles on my right hand are bruised and bloody, and I wonder what Simon's face looks like.

There are four chairs set up in the front yard for the parade, and at first I think how fucked up it is that Mum and Dad put out a chair for Trixie, but then I remember that Dana was going to watch the parade with us.

Until she found me on the porch with Lucy's head on my lap.

The Watermelon Days parade is a big deal—the whole town comes out for it, and we've always had a front row seat. It's the first time I've seen Mum and Dad together in days. Dad's got his shit together. He's had a shave and a shower and is wearing clean clothes.

"Hello, sweetie," Mum says as I sit down in the lawn chair next to her. "What on earth happened to your hand, Ben? And your eye is swollen!"

"I'm okay, Mum, it's nothing," I tell her.

"It's not nothing! Were you fighting?"

When I don't say anything, Dad jumps in. "Your mother asked you a question, Ben."

"Look," I say. I'm tired and hungover and my head's pounding. "Can we just skip all this and go right to the part where I say I'm sorry and I promise not to do it again?"

"Oh, Ben," Mum says, and my gut twists. I hate to disappoint her, but I hated that smug look on Simon's face more.

After a minute or two of silence, Mum asks, "Where's Dana?"

"She's not coming."

She reaches into the cooler and hands me a bottle of iced tea. "Not coming? Why ever not?"

"We're done," I mumble.

"Do you mean you've broken up?"

"That's right." I take a long drink of the tea. I hadn't realized how thirsty I was.

"I'm sorry to hear that," Mum says. "That seems a bit sudden."

I don't say anything as a couple of fire trucks blast their horns. The firefighters throw candy out the windows, and the kids in front of us scramble to get a few pieces. Something flies at me, and I reach up to catch it without thinking, without even looking.

I open my palm. A root beer barrel.

Trixie's favorite candy. The candy Lucy left on her grave. I wonder how often Lucy goes there to visit my sister.

I wonder how often Lucy gets drunk like she did last night.

I think about how it felt to carry Lucy from the shore to the porch, how light she was, how she rested her head against my shoulder. I flex my fingers into a fist and remember the feel of Simon Stanford's shoulder and chest and face beneath it as I pummeled him. What a fucking ass, the thing he said about Lucy.

And then it hits me, like I'm the one getting pounded. What if it's true?

What if Lucy slept with him? Last night I figured he was lying to me, trying to piss me off. And it worked. But maybe he was telling the truth.

My stomach turns. Shit, what if it's true? How could she do that?

God, I'm a hypocrite.

"I saw Lucy and her friend down by the café," Mum says. "Why don't you ask them to join us here? You've spoken with her, right? Like you promised?"

I stand up.

I bite my lip.

"I can't." My voice shakes. "I can't ask her over here. What's done is done and there's no going back."

"Ben—" Mum starts, but I cut her off.

"I've done some really stupid shit since Trixie died, you know?" I can barely get the words out, and I'm glad that the siren of the ambulance in the parade is loud enough that the dozens of spectators around us won't hear what I'm about to say. "I'm sorry that I disappointed you."

I walk away, away from the parade and the noise and my parents, up the hill to the cemetery, to Trixie's grave.

I pull the root beer barrel out of my pocket, unwrap it, and set it on top of her gravestone.

"Trix," I tell her, "I've fucked everything up."

46 · Lucy

THE LAST OF THE PARADE FLOATS PASS US. THE BOY SCOUTS hit the street and sidewalk to pick up the missed candy and trash. Hannah waves her watermelon-shaped paper fan in front of her face.

"It's hot," she says. "Ready to go?"

"Sure." I stand up. As we walk down the block, I see Jane and Tom in their yard, folding up lawn chairs.

I'm filled with a rush of emotions—sadness and regret and the bitter ache of missing them.

I don't want to miss them anymore.

"Hannah," I say, "how would you like to meet Trixie's parents?"

She grins at me and pulls me into a tight hug. "Lucille, I can't think of anything I'd rather do! Except maybe Guthrie." She laughs and I roll my eyes.

We walk across the street and she squeezes my hand. "You can do this," she whispers, and I'm so grateful for her my heart might split in two.

"Lucy," Jane says as she stands, "it's so wonderful to see you."

And before I know what I'm doing, I'm in her arms, tears dampening the shoulder of her blouse. When I finally pull myself away, Tom is standing, too, and puts his hand on my arm.

"We've missed you, kiddo," he says.

I remember that Hannah is here, too, and I step back to include her.

"Jane, Tom, this is my friend, Hannah Mills. Hannah, meet Trixie's mum and dad."

Hannah—awesome, fearless, incomparable Hannah—hugs them both. "I've been waiting a long time to meet y'all," she says. "I've heard a lot about Trixie, and I'm so sorry for your loss."

Jane nods like she might cry and reaches for my hand. "Thank you," she says.

"I know Ben, too," Hannah says. "I'm dating Scott Guthrie."

Oh, I wish she hadn't brought up Ben.

"Yes, Scott mentioned you," Jane says. "Girls, why don't you come inside where it's cool and have some iced tea?"

"We'd love to," Hannah says. She nods at me, as if she's telling me I can do this. It's going to be hard, but I can do this.

I help Tom carry the lawn chairs to the garage.

"Lucy, you have no idea how happy we are that you're here," Tom says as he holds the door for me and I step into the kitchen. I take a deep breath. I haven't been here since Trixie died.

It feels likes home, like no time has passed at all.

As we're walking back up the hill to Hannah's car, I get a text from Mom. *Still in town? Stop by for some pie.*

I hold out the phone to Hannah. "Seems suspicious. Code for *We're up to our eyeballs, come help.*"

"Oh, Lucille," Hannah says, "don't be so hard on her. Go on, see what she's up to."

"You don't think I'm going to go in there alone, do you? Come with me."

"No way. I haven't seen Guthrie for days. I need me some sugar."

"Days? It's only been a few hours!"

She laughs. "It feels like days. Meet us at the carnival later? Text me when you're done."

She hugs me, and I turn to walk back down the hill to the restaurant. This is the second full day of their soft open—Mom wanted to be back in business by Watermelon Days but hasn't had her big grand-reopening celebration yet. It's not as busy as I expect. Most of the parade crowd must have worked its way back to the festival grounds or the lake.

I slide into the booth across from Mom. From here I can see Trixie's quote in swirling script on the chalkboard wall by the door: *Life is no "brief candle" for me. It is a sort of splendid torch which I have got hold of for the moment, and I want to make it burn as brightly as possible.*

Mom's got a notebook in front of her, filled with lists and figures. She refills her coffee cup from the carafe on the table and offers me some. I shake my head.

"What's up?" I ask. "Do you need me to work or something?"

She frowns. "That's what you automatically think, isn't it?"

I shrug. "Well. Yes. I mean, isn't that what you usually want?"

She nods. "I'm sorry for that. And I do have a favor to ask, but that can wait."

Joellen sets a glass of water in front of me. "What can I get you girls?" she asks.

Mom shakes her head. "I'm fine. Luce? Pie?"

I haven't eaten much today besides the banana and a cookie with Jane and Tom, but the combination of Advil and sunshine and Hannah seems to have worked. My stomach growls.

"Wild rice burger, pub style, onion rings. And a Coke. And a slice of lemon meringue."

My mom raises her eyebrows at me. "You must be feeling better."

I shrug. "Yes and no. I suppose Dad filled you in?"

"Yes."

"Is *that* why I'm here? So you can lecture me? Trust me, Dad's was sufficient."

I don't expect her to laugh, but she does. "I'm sure it was."

"So what, then?"

"Are you okay, sweetheart?"

"What do you mean?"

"Well, I mean that it's been a rough year for you, and you've been so distant this summer, and I just want to make sure that everything's okay with you."

My mouth drops open. I can't help it. There's so much I could tell her, but she continues before I can say a word.

"I know it's been a lot different around home now that I'm running this place. And with Clayton at school. Your dad and I have had to figure out a lot of things financially, and it hasn't been easy."

"I know."

"I appreciate everything you do to help out around the house, Lucy, and here, too. You're one of my best servers."

"I am?"

"Yes. People love you. You work so well under pressure, you're never ruffled when it gets busy, and you treat everyone like your guest. I'm proud of you. I know I don't tell you that often enough."

"Wow. I mean, thanks."

She laughs, then smiles sadly. "Losing Trixie was hard on us, too, Luce. It's hard to see someone close to you lose a child. It was easier for me to throw myself into the restaurant. But then this place burned, and I realized that you can rebuild a restaurant, start again. Other losses are . . . irreplaceable. When Shay asked me how you were doing with the anniversary coming up, and I couldn't answer her, I felt terrible."

This is a lot to take in. "Shay?"

"Yes." She takes a sip of coffee. "Simon told her about Trixie and the anniversary, and she asked me how you were doing with it. I had no answer. Luce, I'm so sorry."

When I don't say anything, she continues. "It's okay to be sad, Lucy. It's okay to miss her. I hope you know that your dad and I are here for you if you need us."

It's nice to hear her say this after some of the conversations we've had this summer. I nod. "I know."

Joellen sets my food down and laughs as I dig into the pie first.

Mom smiles and reaches across the table to pat my hand. "Now, I need a favor. Can you work Monday? It's our big Grand Reopening, you know, with a ribbon cutting from the Chamber of Commerce and everything. Louis from the paper will be there. Clayton's coming home for it."

"Seriously?"

"Yes, and Dad took the day off. I'd like for the whole family to be there."

"But you need me to work?"

"You're as much a part of this place as anyone."

"No problem," I tell her. "What time?"

"No problem?" she repeats. "Who are you and what have you done with my daughter?"

"Ha ha."

Mom reaches across the table again, this time for an onion ring. "So, tell me about Simon."

I roll my eyes and take another bite of pie. "Don't invite Simon and Shay to the Grand Opening, okay?" I mumble through a mouthful of meringue. "I'm going to break up with him."

"I thought you liked him."

My phone buzzes with Simon's name at the top of the screen. "Speak of the devil," I mutter.

My grandpa died today. We're on our way home. I won't be back for a few days.

My breath rushes out of me, awful feelings of relief and guilt. "Oh."

"What's wrong?" Mom asks.

"Simon's grandfather died."

Her eyes go soft. "That's terrible."

I tap out a quick reply. *Simon, I'm so sorry.*

I set my phone aside. There isn't much else to say.

47 · Ben

When I get home from the cemetery, Mum's clearing glasses and a tray of cookies off the table.

"Hey," I say to her back, and when she turns from the sink, she has a huge smile on her face.

"Ben, thank you." She sets down the tray. "Thank you so much." She hugs me tight.

For what? I count the glasses. Four.

"Um, did you have company?"

"Yes," she says, and finally lets me go. "Lucy and her delightful friend, Hannah."

"What?"

"They popped over after the parade. Thank you, Ben, for clearing things up with Lucy. I hope that you'll be able to be friends with her again."

I stare at her, dumbfounded.

I think back to last night. Did I say something to Lucy? Did I apologize to her? I was drunk, yes, but not drunk enough to not remember every single thing I did or said.

Or what was said to me.

"Did she say that I did?" I ask.

"No, darling, I'm sure it was awkward for her." Mum smiles again. "We had a wonderful visit."

It's been a long time since I've seen her this happy.

God, I'm a real piece of shit for a son. All those days she

couldn't get out of bed, all the times she sat in Trixie's room and cried, all those hours she spent in her garden, missing her dead daughter—would those days have been better if I hadn't been such a shit to Lucy and kept her away?

I take a deep breath. I should tell her that I didn't say a word to Lucy, that I haven't kept my promise.

Lucy came back on her own.

"That's nice, Mum," I say.

"Are you okay, Ben? You seemed upset when you left."

Am I okay? I think I'm better, at least. "Mum, I'll be in my room, okay?"

But I don't make it that far. Trixie's door is open, the late afternoon sun streaming across the floor. There's a fresh vase of wildflowers on her desk.

I haven't set foot in here since before Trixie died.

But I do now.

I walk into her room, over to her bed, crisply made, half a dozen decorative pillows propped up against the headboard. Her alarm clock, an empty glass, two unwrapped butterscotch candies, a paperback copy of *The Outsiders* facedown and splayed open to the page where she'd stopped reading. Lucy always scolded her when she did that.

I turn to the window, run my finger along the sill. There is no dust.

Trixie's desk is cluttered, papers and pencils and books scattered across its surface. A bulletin board above the desk is filled with movie ticket stubs, postcards, photos of her and Lucy through the years. School dances, with Emily, at the beach, on the pontoon.

In all these photos, Trixie's face is lit and sparkling and wild, and that light carries across to Lucy's.

I peer closer, to one of the two of them at the Aerial Lift Bridge in Duluth last summer, and I can see that I'm wrong. I remember Lucy's excitement, her joy, and I realize that the light of her smile is her very own.

They were good for each other, those two.

Lucy was good for me, too.

A composition notebook lies on the corner of Trixie's messy desk. I recognize it, the notebook that Trix and Lucy scribbled in constantly.

The words *The Book of Quotes* stretch across the cover, written in blue bubble letters.

I sit down at the desk and gently open its tattered cover. Colorful letters fill each page, each quote written with a different, bold-hued marker. Song lyrics. Movie quotes. Funny things they said to each other. Long passages from *The Great Gatsby*, Jane Austen. Sketches and doodles fill the edges of the pages: flowers and stars and hearts.

I hold on to the words that my sister loved enough to write them down. I feel closer to her here, in her room, the same as it was the day she left us, everything exactly as it was that last morning she lived.

She died doing what she loved best. She died in the lake she loved.

I turn another page and there, in bold purple letters, Trixie wrote this:

Life is short, so live it.

I can almost hear her say the words the day I bought the Firebird.

Her life was short, but she did—she lived it.

I close the notebook and set it back down on the desk, feeling a familiar sinkhole in my gut.

She's never coming back.

She's never coming back.

I didn't get to her in time.

I sit at her desk, my head in my hands, and choke back a sob.

Life is short, so live it.

Ever since that day, I haven't been living my life, not really. I've blamed myself and numbed the pain and wasted time.

I won't do it anymore.

I *can't* do it anymore.

I stand, push in the chair, walk to the door. But I stop, turn back, and grab the book.

It doesn't belong here.

Lucy should have it, this artifact of her friendship with my sister.

A couple of hours later, I get a text from Guthrie to meet him at the carnival. I assume he'll be there with Hannah, and I want to ask him if Lucy's going to be there, but I don't. What would I do anyway? Not go?

I'm going to go, whether she's there or not. This is the Watermelon Days carnival. I've never missed one.

I've never missed one and neither had Trixie. Like the parade that we always watched from our front yard.

Another first. My first Watermelon Days carnival without my sister.

I see Guthrie and the girls at the mini-donut stand, lit up bright and cheerful against the dusky night sky. I stop, shove my hands into the pockets of my jeans, and take a deep breath.

How much does Lucy remember about last night? If she didn't remember that I beat up her boyfriend, I'm sure she knows by now.

But Simon's not here. I wouldn't guess he'd show his face, for a couple of reasons.

There's a twinge at the base of my stomach as she looks up from her bag of mini-donuts, one held between two fingers, catches my eye, and looks away quickly. Guthrie sees me, too, and lifts up his hand in a half wave. I move my feet again. Hannah smiles, first at Lucy and then at me.

"Hey," Guthrie says. "You made it."

I nod. Hannah loops one arm through mine and one through Guthrie's. "Lucy has to be home by eleven, so let's do this."

Lucy doesn't say a word, not to me, not to anyone.

I can't believe it, but Hannah convinces her to go on a ride. Last year she could only handle the Ferris wheel—the worst if you're afraid of heights, I think—and the rest of the night, I stayed behind with her while Guthrie and Trixie and Clayton and the others hit every one, some two or three times.

"Go on the rides, Ben," she said while we waited in line for the ring toss. "You don't have to stop having fun because of me."

"I'm having fun," I said. "Are you kidding me? What's more fun than the ring toss?"

I smiled at her then, and she looked up at me and smiled, too, and it would have been so easy to lean down and kiss her and show her how I felt about her.

But I didn't, and Clayton appeared out of nowhere then to tell us where everyone had ended up for the fireworks.

Now, after the first ride, she steps off the car and says, "I—I think I'm going to go home."

Hannah frowns. "No, Lucille, not yet! It's only 9:30! It's not even dark yet, not really. Come on, stay."

Lucy shakes her head. "Really, I can't stay. This— this is the first carnival without Trixie, you know?" She says this in almost a whisper, but I hear it. She feels it, too.

I expect Hannah to say something like *It's time to accept it* or *She's gone, there's nothing you can do,* those terrible things people say, people who don't understand.

Instead she pulls Lucy into a hug. "I get it. This is a sad day for you. We'll take you home."

Lucy shakes her head again. "No, don't be stupid. I can walk."

"You're not walking home by yourself! Guthrie, tell her we'll take her home."

"I can take her," I say. I don't know where it comes from.

Hannah and Guthrie both look at me, surprised, but Lucy doesn't. She won't look at me. I don't blame her.

"No," Lucy says. "I want to walk home. It's fine. I'll be fine."

I reach out and put my hand on her arm. Now, finally, she looks up at me, her eyes wide. "I'll take you home."

She nods and hands the rest of her ride tickets to Hannah.

"Text me when you get home, Lucille," Hannah says, "so I know you're safe."

Lucy starts walking.

She's not arguing with me. She's letting me help her.

She's not pushing me away.

There's a twinge again, but this time, it's not guilt. It's hope.

48 · Lucy

WHAT IS WRONG WITH ME?

I'm still not one hundred percent on everything that happened with Ben at the party last night, and now I've just told him he can give me a ride home. Or didn't tell him he couldn't, I guess. My stomach churns with anxiety and the leftover effects of the Hurricane ride.

Once we get to the mini-donut stand, I'll stop and tell him I changed my mind. That I can't get in the car with him.

But we pass the mini-donut stand, and I don't say a word.

When we get to the Zipper, I'll tell him. I'll say, "You know what? It's fine, I'm fine, just go back and have fun."

But we pass the Zipper, too, the screams of its riders cutting into my thoughts.

The gate. I'll tell him at the gate.

And then we're out of the gate, walking down the street toward his house. It's quieter outside the carnival grounds, quieter still as we walk away, except for occasional laughter or the rev of an engine.

It will take us three minutes to walk to his house, maybe less.

I'll tell him in the driveway.

He's so close to me. His footsteps and mine are in sync as we walk together. I don't notice anything around me except for his closeness and his warmth and his smell. Tonight he doesn't smell like the lake or sunscreen or fish. He smells fresh, like soap, and sweet, like the cinnamon sugar of mini-donuts.

He pulls his keys out of his pocket as we walk up the driveway. He opens the passenger door for me, and I'm so overcome by the rush of emotion that my knees buckle.

He reaches out to steady me.

His fingers on my arm are too much.

"Ben," I say, but still, I won't look at his face. This is when I will tell him that I can't get in the car, that I've changed my mind.

"Please let me take you home," he says, his voice so low and plaintive, I want to cry.

"Have you been drinking?" I ask, like that's the reason I don't want to get in the car with him. I bite my lip to keep from crying, trying to make it seem like I'm being practical, logical, like this has nothing to do with the last time—the only time—I sat in the front seat of the Firebird.

He shakes his head. "No," he says, and now he sounds pissed. "No, I haven't been drinking."

I know he's telling the truth. I can see it when I finally let myself look into his eyes, and they are clear, and flashing in the light from the streetlamp, and filled with pain.

He's in your heart, Hannah said.

He is. I want to see if we can salvage what we might have had, but standing here, next to the open passenger door of the Firebird, I can't. I remember every word that he said to me in that car. Every word.

I can't. I can't get into the Firebird. I can't let Ben help me.

"I don't need your help." My voice cracks. "I'll walk home."

"Why don't you ask your boyfriend for a ride, then?" The anger is still there, hovering beneath the surface of Ben's words, and his expression changes. Tight, closed, pissed off. "Where is he, anyway?"

I pinch my lips together. It's none of his business where Simon is, and my stomach twists when I think about the reason he's not here. "He went back to St. Paul," I snap. "His grandfather died. And thanks to you, I'm sure he looks like shit."

"Not my problem," he says.

"What is wrong with you? Why would you do that to him? To anyone? I don't know you anymore, Ben."

I stare at him, see an almost imperceptible shift of his jaw. He won't say anything. I turn away from him and hurry down the driveway.

That wisp of a memory of Ben's fingers in my hair at Hannah's party must have been my imagination.

Nothing has changed.

49 · Ben

I slam the door of the Firebird, rev the engine, and back out. I drive in the opposite direction of downtown and Lucy, past Lions Park and the carnival. I drive until my eyes blur.

The peace, the resolve I felt this afternoon are gone.

Why can't I get Lucy out of my head? I've been able to kill my emotions for months, and the minute I see her at the resort, I'm lost.

Guthrie thinks I'm on the right path. Isn't that what he meant that night on the beach? Lucy's the right path. She's been the right path all along, and I've been too fucking stupid to see it.

And she's right, I am an asshole.

I am a stupid, fucking asshole, and it seems like all I know how to do is hurt the person I love the most.

I've hurt her so much, so many times.

And, God, Trixie would be so pissed at me for this, for all of this. For pushing Lucy away when I should have held her close. For all those other girls I've hooked up with. Trixie would shake her head and smirk and whack me on the arm.

"Fix it, Ben," she would say. "Don't let her go."

Life is short, so live it.

I pull off the road. I turn around in the weedy parking lot of the abandoned Bump 'n' Putt on 371 and head for home.

For Lucy.

If I hurry, I can catch her.

And she's still there, out on the county road past Sullivan Street Park, walking on the shoulder. It's busy and dark and the cars fly past her. She's going to get herself killed if she's not careful.

I won't let that happen.

I slam on the brakes, pull over.

I never should have let her go.

50 · Lucy

I'M ABOUT A HALF MILE PAST THE GAS-N-GO WHEN I HEAR the crunch of tires on the gravel of the shoulder behind me. The car stops but I do not.

"Lucy!"

I stop walking.

It's Ben.

Ben.

He's here.

"Lucy," he says again. He reaches me in an instant, turns me toward him, his hand on my arm. "Let me drive you home. You'll get yourself killed."

I can't look at him. I look down at my sandals, the gravel.

"I'm fine." I'm so tired of this. "I don't need a ride. I told you that."

"Please get in the car," he says.

"No, I can't go with you."

"Get in the fucking car." He sounds frustrated. "Stop playing this game."

"What game?"

He doesn't answer my question. "Just get in the car!"

I wrench my arm away from him. Now I'm angry. I'm so mad at him for everything he's done and hasn't done since Trixie died.

"How about your game?" I snap. "The game where you're

so nice to me one minute and the next, you're a complete dick? Or how about the one where you sleep with every girl who thinks she can save you? Fuck you."

That shuts him up. His mouth drops open.

"What?" I say. "Why do you seem so surprised? I've watched you, Ben. You eat up their sympathy."

His mouth closes, then opens again like he's going to say something.

I want him to say something. I want him to tell me that he's sorry, that he misses me, that he loves me. I want him to take back every terrible thing he said to me after Trixie's funeral.

He knew. He knew how much I liked him, that I had for years, and he pushed me away. He knew. He knew when we were in Duluth last summer—how could he not have known?

I screw up my courage. "How long have you known how much I liked you, Ben?" *Loved you. I have always loved you.* "A long time?"

There's a flicker in his eyes. He nods.

"And you—did you like me, too? What were you going to say to me just before—"

"Lulu." He cuts me off, his voice low and certain. He moves toward me, and his mouth is on mine and his arms circle around my back and he pulls me close. We stand in the gravel on the side of the road and cars *whoosh* past us and he kisses me, urgent and seeking, and his tongue slips into my mouth and oh, God, it's so much. Everything.

I reach my arms up around his neck, twist my fingers into

his curls, and pull him closer to me. I press my body up against his. I can never be close enough to him. Everywhere we touch, electricity and warmth course through me. I'm alive, I'm living.

This is what I've waited for since that day, the day of Trixie's funeral. I've waited for him to come back to me. Waited for the impossible.

But not like this. Not like this, so close to the anniversary, when we're both so sad and angry.

What are we doing?

I slide my arms down, against his chest, and shove him back. He gasps as I step away.

"Lu?" There's hurt in his voice, but I can't let it get to me. I can't.

"No. Not like this."

"What is that supposed to mean?"

I want to hurt him like he hurt me.

"Isn't this your usual routine? You're sad, some girl wants to save you from your sadness, you get laid?"

His mouth drops open again, like he can't believe what he's hearing. And I can't believe I'm saying it. His eyes bore into me, wide and wounded. "Lulu, no," he says, and takes a step toward me.

I hold up my hands to stop him. "Leave me alone, Ben. I can't save you."

I walk away and let the tears fall. I've gone a few yards when I hear the car door slam, hear the Firebird rev and peel out. In the other direction. Away from me.

51 · Ben

THIS IS NOT THE RIGHT PATH.

52 · *Lucy*

THE NEXT DAY, I WAKE WITH THE MEMORY OF BEN'S ARMS around me, of his kiss. How I pushed him away. My stomach drops.

It wasn't supposed to be like this.

My parents are at work, and the empty, echoing house closes in on me. I step out to the deck. The sky today is sunny, bright blue. A bluebird sky, Ben would call it.

I wonder what Ben's doing, if he's out fishing, if he's thinking of me and the horrible things I said.

I call Hannah.

"Lucille," she says after I've told her what happened, "honey, you've got to let him back in."

If only it were that easy.

I get ready for work.

At the Full Loon, I can be one of my mom's best servers. I can treat every customer like a guest. I can throw myself into it. I can ignore the sick feeling in my stomach, the guilt that bubbles up. Guilt about the kiss. Guilt about feeling so relieved that Simon has gone home for his grandfather's funeral, that I don't have to see his bruised face.

Everyone in town comes out for the Grand Reopening the next day. Tami brings Emily, who spins on one of the new stools at the counter. Clayton shows up as promised. He hugs me and says, "So, how's my favorite little delinquent?" I shove him but really I'm glad to see him.

We serve pie and coffee. The man from the newspaper takes pictures and interviews Mom and Daniel. We all crowd around behind the red ribbon as Mom cuts it with an enormous pair of silver shears. Rita's here even though she quit months ago—Mom said it wouldn't be the same without her.

And later, because it's Monday night, Guthrie and Ben show up.

They sit at the counter and my mom serves them. Guthrie raises his hand in a wave as I walk into the kitchen.

I shiver, remembering Ben's hands on my back as he pulled me close to him, his lips on mine.

"Take these out to the boys?" Daniel says, motioning to two plates of the Grand Reopening Special—Daniel's brand-new Five Alarm Jalapeño Burger with Smoky Sweet Potato Wedges.

"The boys?"

"Yeah. Ben and Guthrie, at the counter?"

"I'm not on the counter tonight, Daniel," I tell him. My voice shakes, and I'm irritated with myself for being such a baby.

"Patty's out having a smoke. I'd take them myself but I got my hands full back here. Come on, Luce."

"Fine," I snap. I can do this.

When I bring out their plates, Guthrie says, "The place looks great, Luce. Even better than before."

"Thanks," I tell him. "Can I get you guys anything else?"

Guthrie mumbles no, his mouth already stuffed with sweet potato wedges. I feel Ben's eyes on me, and when I turn to him, he holds my gaze and I can't move. There is so much hurt in his eyes. I can't bear to look at him.

"Lucy!" I hear Daniel call from the kitchen. "Order up!"

I turn away before Ben can see my tears.

Three days later, Simon comes back.

When I get home from work, Dad says, "Shay stopped by. She said Simon's pretty upset. She asked if you'd go over when you got home."

"Okay," I mumble. "Sure."

I'll go. Of course I'll go. Simon's still my boyfriend. And he's hurting.

I'd planned to talk to him soon anyway, for a different reason. This—being with him when he's grieving—might be harder than telling him that I need to break up with him.

Now I know how people must feel around me.

I walk across the small grassy patch between our houses. Shay answers the door.

"Oh, Lucy," she says and pulls me into her chest. "Thank you for coming over."

"I'm very sorry for your loss, Shay."

"Simon's downstairs. He'll be so glad to see you."

There's something in her voice that tells me she wants me to find a way to help him.

I don't know how, really. But one thing I do know: Grief takes its time.

Simon sleeps in the basement. I haven't been here much this summer, and I haven't set foot in his bedroom, but I know my way around the Clarks' house as well as my own. His door is closed, so I knock. He doesn't answer or invite me in, but I open the door slowly and walk across the room.

The room is dark except for the bright blue glow of a neon clock above the dresser. Music plays from an iPod dock on the desk, Pink Floyd, "Wish You Were Here." Clothes are thrown across the back of an old recliner in the corner, and there's a stack of Stephen King paperbacks on the nightstand.

Simon's lying on top of the covers, his hands linked across his stomach, and his even breaths carry across the room. He's asleep.

I step closer to the bed. His hair's its usual mess, and except for the fading bruises, his face looks so peaceful, so calm. You'd never know that someone important to him had died, that inside of him, his heart and his soul have withered with the news.

I know what it's like. I know what he's feeling. I wheel the office chair from his desk over to the bed. I sit. The music changes to a song I don't recognize, melancholy and aching.

Like everything in this room.

Simon stirs and startles when he opens his eyes and sees me.

"Lucy," he says. "I've been waiting for you." He reaches out a hand for mine, and it's warm and soft against my skin.

"I'm so sorry about your grandfather, Simon."

He nods and his eyes fill with tears.

"I'm not ready to believe it yet," he murmurs. He props himself up on his elbows like he's about to sit up. "Not even after the funeral."

"No," I tell him. "Sleep. I'll stay here with you."

He smiles, but it's not the wide grin that I'm used to.

He's hurt.

"You know, don't you?" he says. "You know what this feels like."

I nod.

"I'm glad you're here." He scoots to the side of the bed, making room for me. I lie down close to him and put my arm across his chest. He's warm, and I can feel his heart beat. He turns to face me. "Thank you."

I shouldn't be here.

It's not long before he falls back asleep.

I remember the days right after Trixie died, when I couldn't get out of bed, my body so heavy, exhausted by the grief coursing through me. While I was sleeping, I didn't have to think. I didn't have to think about what happened the day Trixie died or Ben's words that echoed through my head. I slept until I couldn't sink any further into my grief, I moved through the days on autopilot, I prayed that I would wake up and the pain of missing her would have dissipated in my slumber.

Simon stirs again, murmurs a word I can't make out. I brush my fingers against the hair that lies across his forehead.

I let him sleep. I let him feel comforted.

The next time I see him will be different.

53 · Ben

It's quiet at the resort today—there aren't a lot of kids here this week. One of the cabins has rented out the pontoon for the day. A group of sisters and their daughters in Bear and Wolf are spread out on the loungers at the beach. I hang out at the lodge and wait for someone to come in to play pool or buy snacks but no one does. At three o'clock I close up the lodge and do the garbage run, then go over to Loon to start cleanup.

Loon's the smallest cabin, a studio with a small bathroom. The resort is usually sold out all summer, but this year they haven't rented out Loon as much. John decided to add on a loft bedroom, so they're closing it up for the last two weeks of summer to get started on renovations.

This is good. I need the quiet, I need to be alone.

Lucy's not here today.

Monday night, seeing her at the Full Loon, was a kick in the gut. I think of how she pushed me away when I kissed her and what Simon told me the night of Hannah's party.

Lucy slept with Simon.

And she doesn't want to be with me.

I start in the kitchenette, cleaning out the small refrigerator. The stuff guests leave behind—mustard, half-empty milk jugs, tubs of butter.

The guy who rented Loon last week left a couple of cans of beer in the fridge. No sense in wasting those. Perfect. I'll drink away every fucking thing that's happened this summer, Lucy and Simon and what an asshole I've been. I'm about to crack one open, but something stops me.

John and Tami trust me. I shouldn't drink on the job.

All this time, I've been killing everything with booze—all my guilt and regret, all the sorrow that's been eating away at me. And it hasn't changed one fucking thing. Trixie's still dead.

But Lucy's not. She's right here.

God, if I could just think of a way to fix it.

I put the beer in a plastic bag I find under the sink and throw it in the back of the UTV.

I've screwed up a lot of shit this summer, but I'm not going to screw this up. It's a start.

When I get back up to the lodge, Dad and John are playing pool. John takes a shot and sinks the eight ball, game over.

"Why don't you two knock off?" he says. "No sense in hanging around when it's this slow."

"I guess," I say.

Dad puts his cue in the rack and turns to me. "What do you say we hit up the weeds?"

I'm about to say no when I catch his eye. There's something different about him today.

His eyes are clear. Bright.

"You thinking walleye?" I ask. It's August, hot and humid, some say a slow month for fishing. Not my dad. You just gotta know where to look.

"Yeah, why not?" he says.

Why not?

Dad and I spend the next three hours out on the edge of the weeds. We don't snag any walleye, but we get a couple of nice bass and a few northerns.

Neither one of us says much, but just before Dad pulls up anchor, I ask, "How many days has it been?"

He doesn't look at me when he answers. "Four. Friday night was the last. Went to a meeting up at the church last night."

Four. He hasn't had a drink in four days. He went to an AA meeting.

"What changed?" I'm almost afraid to know.

He doesn't answer right away. And then, "Me, I guess. I took a long look at myself, and I didn't much like what I saw. I had to stop blaming myself for what happened to Trixie, for not knowing that she was sick. And I realized that I'm the only one who gets to decide."

"Decide what?"

"How I'm going to get through this. And it can go either way, so why not make the best of it?"

I expect him to segue into a lecture about how if I'm not careful, I'll end up a drunk like him, in denial, but he doesn't. Instead, he says, "You have to stop blaming yourself, Ben. And living without your sister? It might not get easier, but it will get different."

I nod. I think I know what he means. Different. It could go either way. And I'm the only one who can choose how I'm going to get through it.

At home, I open up my laptop for the first time all summer. It takes me almost an hour to find exactly what I need. I pull Lucy and Trixie's notebook from my desk drawer and open it to the first blank page I find. And then I write the quote I found. I want to say more. I want to explain everything, but I don't. I write a few more words, sign my name.

I hope it's enough.

I put the notebook and one of my unpolished agates— rough, but still beautiful—in a brown paper bag and write Lucy's name on it with a marker. I walk back to the resort. The late afternoon heat presses down on me. I feel the sting of Lulu's rejection, but it doesn't slow my steps. A lull has settled over the resort and there's no one to see as I climb the rickety ladder of the tree house and put the paper bag in the corner.

My peace offering.

54 · *Lucy*

"Lucy! Lucy!"

I hear Emily's call from the tree house across the yard and I speed up, my heart pounding. It's not panic, but I am up the ladder in seconds, not bothering to worry about the loose boards or the height.

"What's wrong?" I ask, out of breath.

She's grinning, pointing at a plain brown bag.

"It's for you!" she says. "A mysterious package!" She doesn't pronounce *mysterious* correctly, slipping the last syllables together, and I smile.

"You scared me," I tell her, and I pull her to me in a hug before I move to the bag.

My name is there, in heavy letters, all caps, slanted to the left.

Ben's handwriting.

I think about his kiss on the side of the road, the look he gave me at the Full Loon, and again, my heart's in my throat.

"Aren't you going to open it?" Emily tugs on my hand.

"Oh, yes, of course." I kneel down, pick up the package. It weighs almost nothing. The paper crinkles as I open it.

Our notebook. The Book of Quotes. And something else— an agate.

"An old notebook?" Emily asks, obviously disappointed. "And a *rock*?"

When I look at her, she is a watery blur.

I'm crying.

I open the cover, run my finger over the familiar letters.

"It was mine and Trixie's," I manage to tell her.

"Oh," she says, like she understands, and I believe that she does. She sits down next to me, takes my hand, and squeezes it. "It's okay, Lucy," she says. "Crying will make you feel better." It does.

And when I've stopped crying, I look through the notebook, page by page, and soon I'm laughing, caught up in the memories.

Trixie, studying for a humanities exam: *My head hurts like Aristotle when he was thinking.*

Trixie, cleaning out her hamster Ethel's cage: *I can't tell what's shit and what's raisins.*

Me, one afternoon at the Full Loon: *You can tell a lot about a person by the kind of pie they order. Mainly if they're assholes or not.*

One of the most beautiful qualities of true friendship is to understand and to be understood. —Seneca

My breath catches when I turn to the last of the filled-in pages.

The handwriting matches my name on the brown paper bag.

One word frees us of all the weight and pain of life: That word is love. —Sophocles

And below it: *Lulu, please forgive me. I love you. —Ben.*

I touch the inky words, my heart racing. Ben found the

notebook, wrote his love in the pages, and brought it back to me. I'm filled with a rush of lightness. Forgiveness.

I love him. No matter what.

It's time to let him back in.

I need to break up with Simon tonight.

I call Simon when I get home from the resort.

"I'm sorry I was so out of it last night," he says. "Can you do something tonight?"

"Yes. Can you come over here?"

"Let's go out for pie," he says. "I'm really going to miss that pie."

The Full Loon isn't the ideal location for this conversation, but I can wait until the drive home.

I meet him in the driveway and he hugs me. "I wish you could have been there with me," he says.

I step back out of his arms, thinking of the words Ben wrote in the Book of Quotes, and when we get in the car and Simon reaches for my hand, I pull away, pretending to look for something in my purse.

On the way into town, he talks about his grandfather, the funeral, and how his dad asked him to come back to St. Paul early and fill in at the hardware store until they can hire a full-timer.

"This is my last weekend here. I'm leaving Sunday night, and I won't be back. Not for the rest of the summer, anyway."

I don't say anything. I bite my lip. I'm relieved, but I won't take the easy way out. I have to be honest with him.

He must mistake my silence for sadness, because he says, "I know, babe, I'm going to miss you, too."

My mom is still at the restaurant. It's busy, but there are two stools at the counter. Simon orders a slice of coconut cream, his favorite.

"Nothing for you?" he asks.

I shake my head, but Patty brings me a cup of coffee anyway.

"Lucy, I wanted to talk to you about this fall. My dad's asking how much I'll be able to work at the store, and I told him that it would depend on you."

"On me?"

He nudges me with his shoulder. "Yes, you. You know, if I'll be driving up here on the weekends or if you'll be coming down."

My mouth goes dry. "Coming down?" I somehow say.

"Yeah, to St. Paul? To see me?"

"Oh." It comes out like a sigh. "I, uh. I don't have my license, you know. Or a car."

Mom stops as she walks toward the kitchen, her hands filled with dishes she's just cleared from a table. "Luce, I'm glad you're here. We've got a tour bus coming through in about fifteen minutes—any chance you could help out?"

I'm relieved, so relieved.

"Sure," I say. "I can stay as late as you need."

She smiles. "That would be great. Thanks." She disappears into the kitchen.

But Simon is frowning. "You're going to work?"

"It won't take long, I promise."

"Lucy, I'm leaving Sunday night. For good."

"I know."

"I want to spend as much time with you as possible before then."

"Simon—" I start, but I can't do it here. Not at the Full Loon in front of all these people. I've got to stick with my plan. "Just wait for me, okay? I'll throw on an apron when the bus gets here, and I'll be done in half an hour."

He shakes his head and pushes his plate away. "I can't believe this," he says. "I can't believe you're doing this."

"My mom needs me."

"I need you, too. What's more important, me or the restaurant?"

In that instant, I change my mind.

Now is the time.

"Simon, I know that you're really hurting right now, but there's something I need to tell you." I'm going to do this, right here at the counter at the Full Loon where Ben and Guthrie sat Monday night. "I shouldn't have let you believe that there could ever be anything between us. And I'm sorry for that."

"What do you mean, you let me believe there *could* be something between us? Isn't there something between us, Lucy? I love you."

How many times have I let him say *I love you*?

"I don't love you," I tell him. "And I know that's not fair to you. And—I'm sorry, Simon."

"You're kidding, right?"

I shake my head.

"Oh my God," he says. "This is about Ben, isn't it?"

When I don't say anything, when I don't deny it, he runs his hands through his hair. "I've been so stupid. It was right in front of me the whole time. You're in love with him."

"Yes," I say. "I love Ben. I've loved him for a long time."

"I have to go," he says.

"I'll walk you to your car," I say, and my voice breaks.

He pushes away his plate, the pie untouched, and stands up. He doesn't say a word when I stand up to follow him.

When I turn, my heart leaps into my throat.

Ben and Guthrie are standing in front of me.

Guthrie looks amused, the corners of his mouth twisted up in a smirk. Ben isn't smiling, but his eyes—his eyes are filled with a light I haven't seen in a long time.

And it fills me.

Simon doesn't say anything as we walk out the door, into the parking lot. When we reach his car, I take his hand. He flinches but doesn't let go. It makes no sense to wonder if things could have been different between us. I know the answer. I've hurt us both.

"I'm sorry," I say again in a whisper.

He drops my hand without a word, gets in the Volvo, and drives away.

Good-bye, Simon the Renter.

I need to catch my breath before I go back inside and face Ben, but a tour bus pulls into the lot, and Ben will have to wait.

55 · Ben

Lucy told Simon that she loves me.

Still, after I've treated her like shit for a year, she loves me.

"Well," Guthrie says, "are you going to just stand there or are you going to go after her?"

I've been such an asshole. I lost Trixie but I can't lose Lucy anymore. I love her, I've always loved her, since that first day Trixie brought her home to play. I loved her even then.

I wonder if she saw what I wrote in her notebook. She must have. But I need to tell her in person.

I take a deep breath. It's time to tell her what I was going to say that day on the swim raft at Sullivan Street Park.

It's time to tell her I'm sorry for what I said to her after Trixie's funeral. All the shitty things I've said to her since.

I need to know if she'll forgive me.

But then I see her, coming back in through the kitchen, an apron tied around her waist, an order pad in her hand. She looks at me and shrugs. The front door opens and people stream in—a tour bus. She'll be here all night.

"Damn it," I say.

Guthrie slides onto the stool where Simon had been, unwraps the silverware from the napkin, and starts to eat the untouched pie. "Well, that's done," he says with his mouth full.

Lucy's a blur, moving from table to kitchen and back again. She catches my eye once, then looks away again quickly.

Eventually Guthrie puts money down and says, "We should go. We're taking up valuable real estate here."

I know he's right, but I don't say anything.

"Ben, you heard what she said. That's not going to change before tomorrow."

Tomorrow, the anniversary. Tomorrow I'll find Lucy and ask her to forgive me.

The next morning, I'm up early.

I drive out to Sullivan Street Park. Today I'm going to build a memorial for Trixie, an inuksuk. I've been planning it for weeks, looking for giant rocks around the resort and out at Guthrie's place, keeping them in my trunk. I've got six now and that should be enough—a big one for the base, three medium-size, two smaller ones for the top. They're all of similar shape with flat bottoms. They should stack pretty easily. I've stacked hundreds of rocks since that night at Guthrie's, but nothing like this.

It's pouring rain but it doesn't matter. It should be raining on a day like today. The parking lot at Sullivan Street is empty; technically the park hasn't opened for the day yet. I scoped out the spot for the inuksuk last week—where the grassy part of the park slopes down toward the lake and the woods, at the rocky part of the beach.

I back the Firebird down the grassy hill and stop before the grass ends. One by one I take the rocks from the trunk. The big one must weigh twenty or twenty-five pounds. I nestle it into the rocky sand between the two trees. The next rock, not quite as heavy, sits easily on the flat surface of the bottom one, and in a half hour and without much trouble, all six are balanced and stacked and shine with the rain.

I stand back to look at Trixie's inuksuk. It's nearly as tall as me and stands guard over the lake where Trixie died. Exactly what I wanted. I take another step back. Perfect. It's the most perfect thing I've ever made. It's balanced, controlled, substantial.

"I'm sorry, Trix," I murmur.

I'm jittery from the coffee I downed and building the inuksuk and wondering about Lucy. It's impossible for me to not think about what she told Simon at the Full Loon last night.

After everything I've done, she loves me.

I pull out my phone and scroll through my contacts until I find her name: *Lulu.*

My hands shake as I type: *Can we talk? I'm at the park.*

When she doesn't respond after a few minutes, I send another text.

I'll wait.

56 · Lucy

I SLEEP LATE THE NEXT MORNING, THE ANNIVERSARY OF THE day Trixie died. My feet hurt from a long night at work. I'm tired, but I remember the words Ben wrote. I remember the light in his eyes when he heard me say I loved him.

The hard part is over, isn't it?

Still, I'm nervous, not ready to see him yet.

I make a cup of coffee and take it out to the porch. It's humid and the sky to the west is a murky gray. It will be raining before too long.

My phone buzzes and my heart leaps a little, thinking it might be Ben. It's not. It's Clayton.

Thinking about you & Trix. Sorry I've been such an asswipe lately.

It's the most un-asswipe thing he's done in a long time.

Hannah sends a text, too: *Luv u lucy lucille. I know today is trixies day n want u to know im here if u need me.*

I'm so grateful for her.

I finish my coffee and take a shower. I need to move. I need to move forward.

I walk into town even though the rain has started. My clothes are damp by the time I reach the cemetery.

"Hey, Trix," I say as I sink down onto the bench at her grave.

I fill her in on the rodeo, the grounding, the fire. How Hannah and Guthrie are dating now.

"You should see how cute they are," I tell her. "I don't think I've ever seen Guthrie so happy. And I wish you'd gotten a chance to know Hannah."

I tell her about Simon and what happened in South Dakota. I tell her what Ben wrote in the Book of Quotes and what he heard me say at the Full Loon.

"I haven't seen him, though. And I'm nervous." I laugh. "Isn't that crazy? Your brother told me he loved me, after all this time, and I'm scared to see him, like it's some elaborate joke."

I stand and pull out the crinkly bag of candy I brought for her, translucent green, tied with a dark green ribbon, filled with all of her favorites.

"I love you," I say. "I miss you. Every day. You have no idea how much. You were always there for me, cheering me on. I saw the impossible in every situation, but you knew better. You knew what I had inside of me. I know it now, too."

I place the bag on top of the tombstone.

"Bye, Trix. Sleep well."

The rain has stopped for now, but the humidity hangs heavy in the air. As I turn to leave the cemetery, my phone buzzes with another text.

Can we talk? I'm at the park.

It's what I've been waiting for all morning. Ben. I hurry down the hill toward Sullivan Street Park. I'm still on Main Street when my phone buzzes again: *I'll wait.*

The park is open but nearly empty—a couple of kids on the playground equipment and their parents in the gazebo, and only a few people on the damp beach. Gray, threatening clouds fill the sky.

I see Ben sitting on the sand, his arms around his knees. I stand at the top of the hill for a moment to catch my breath and look out over the lake. The float just outside the swimming area, where we sunned ourselves one year ago today, is empty.

Ben and Clay didn't find Trixie that day. The divers did, hours later.

I've replayed every scenario in my head a million times—if she hadn't raced Clayton, if Ben hadn't stayed on the float with me, if we'd gone to play mini-golf instead, maybe she'd still be alive.

I know this kind of thinking isn't logical. I know that it's not my fault, or Clayton's, or Ben's.

Trixie would have died. If not that day, another. Her heart would have given up on her eventually, and no one knew it.

I close my eyes and breathe in the pungent smell of algae and rain. I open them again and walk down the hill.

When I reach the sand, I notice a tall tower of large rocks behind Ben, as tall as me, one stone balanced on top of another. My chest tightens, and I know Ben made it, and that he made it for Trixie. I'm filled with a rush of emotions. Grief and sadness and relief and missing her so much. And more than anything, love for Ben, who misses her, too.

57 · Ben

THE CHANCE THAT SHE WON'T COME TEARS ME UP. I'M TIRED, AND my muscles ache from lifting the heavy rocks. I sink down into the sand, damp from the rain, and wait.

And then, after what seems like hours, she is there, standing on the beach behind me.

But she's looking past me, to the inuksuk for Trixie, and even from a distance, I can see tears in her eyes. She stands perfectly still on the beach, except even from here, I can see that she's shivering.

Finally, she looks at me. "I got your messages," she says.

I don't think, I just move.

In three strides, I'm where she is, and I take her in my arms.

I hold her, I kiss the top of her head until the shivering stops. She lets me. She's in my arms, and I can keep her warm, and this feels like it was always meant to be. I know, I've always known, that I should be with her, protect her, even though I don't deserve her.

God, I hope she can forgive me. For everything.

"I'm sorry," I say. "I'm sorry."

"I hurt you, too," she murmurs into my shoulder. "I'm so sorry."

"No," I whisper. "Is it true, what you said to Simon? That you love me?"

She nods. She looks up at me and she's crying and I can't handle that. I never want her to cry again.

And then, finally, I lean down to kiss her and she doesn't push me away. She lets me kiss her and hold her and I think, *This is how it's supposed to feel,* and she's really here, she's right here, and she is everything.

"Lu," I say, and her name catches in my throat. "Lulu, you're the only one. I never want us to be apart."

I stand back to look at her, to make sure that she's really here, and her eyes are wide and expectant and scared and oh God, please, let there be forgiveness somewhere there, too.

It's too much. With the others, I felt nothing, going through the motions, all physical, no emotion, no connection. But every time I touch her, I feel something, something electric moving from Lucy's skin to mine, from her blood to mine, from her heart to mine.

Being here with her, standing on this beach in the rain, she is filling me, she is filling some empty part of me.

My breath catches. I fight against a sob.

"Lulu, I have to know if there's a chance for us. I've really screwed things up, and I need to know that you forgive me. Please tell me that you forgive me."

"Yes," she whispers. "Yes. Will you forgive me?"

I lean my forehead against hers, close my eyes, listen for her soft breaths. I am flooded with relief. "There's nothing to forgive, Lulu. I love you."

"Ben," she murmurs. She slips her arms around my waist and we stand like this, not moving, *together*, finally together, for a long moment.

She pulls away and takes my hand, leading me to Trixie's inuksuk.

"You made this," she says. It's not a question.

I nod against the lump in my throat. "Yeah, I miss her."

"It's beautiful," she says. "Perfect."

And then she smiles, and her smile is as bright as the sun that's beginning to break through the clouds. I wrap an arm around her waist and pull her close. She leans her head against my chest.

I never want to let this girl go.

After a few minutes, she says, "What were you going to ask me, Ben? That day on the float?"

I tell her the truth. "I was going to ask you if you wanted to go out on the boat, just you and me. And then, out in the middle of the lake, I was going to ask you to go for a drive. And then to the movies. And when we were at the movies, I was going to ask you if you'd be my girlfriend."

"Oh," she breathes.

"Lulu," I whisper, "Lulu, will you?"

She pulls away to reach into her pocket. She has the agates. Both of them.

She lifts my hand, palm up, and places the stones there. "I love you, Ben. It's always been you."

I link my fingers with hers, the agates between our palms.

"Let's go for a drive," I say.

"Okay," she whispers. "Where should we go?"

I lean in, our hands still clasped, and kiss her, sweetly, tenderly. "Anywhere. Everywhere. Wherever our path leads us."

AUTHOR'S NOTE

THE LAST THING YOU SAID IS A BOOK ABOUT GRIEF, ABOUT healing, about love. The setting and elements of the book were inspired by the world around me, the places and things about Minnesota that I love best.

Setting has always been important to me as a writer, and no place has been as inspiring to me as my home state. Minnesota's landscapes are stunning, from the bluffs along the Mississippi River to the wide expanses of tallgrass prairie to the rocky shores of Lake Superior.

Minnesota also has a rich and varied history, much of which is connected to its landscapes. My father grew up in Pipestone, Minnesota, near the Pipestone National Monument. For centuries, pipestone has been carved into pipes used for prayer, and the site of the historic pipestone quarries is considered sacred by many Native American tribes. My fascination with both Minnesota history and its natural elements began with my visits to Pipestone as a child.

During my college years, I lived in Duluth, a city in northeastern Minnesota along Lake Superior. It was then that I became interested in the history of inuksuit, the stone structures of the Inuit. Although the Inuit are not native to the area, it is not uncommon to see rock structures or sculptures along the North Shore Scenic Highway, in parks throughout the city, or in art galleries. Area sculptors and other artists, musicians, and poets have found inspiration in inuksuit. A massive inuksuk, several feet tall, stands at the Split Rock River Wayside, the trailhead entrance to the Split Rock River Loop of the Superior Hiking Trail. The idea of stone markers as guideposts along life's journey resonated with me, and came to mind when writing about the journey of grief in *The Last Thing You Said.*

Like Ben, I've been collecting rocks for as long as I can remember—agates, stones from the shores of Lake Superior, gemstones, and minerals. I've spent hours searching for agates. I've studied the healing power and spiritual meaning of stones. At my desk, I keep a selenite crystal, said to deliver clarity, that fits in my palm and is worn smooth.

I feel a great connection to the North Shore and the Brainerd Lakes area of Minnesota, and I returned to both places for inspiration many times while writing this book. I haven't lived in Duluth for many years, but nothing soothes my soul more than the sound of Lake Superior waves crashing against the rocky shore. For me, nature holds healing power, and it was only natural that it would, too, for Ben and Lucy.

I hope that someday you'll have an opportunity to visit the Land of 10,000 Lakes, and that you'll love it as much as I do. To learn more about Minnesota, including the history of the Ojibwe and Minnesota's other Native American tribes, visit the Minnesota Historical Society's website at mnhs.org.

ACKNOWLEDGMENTS

I am so very grateful that my lifelong dream of having a book published has come true, and for the support, encouragement, and love from a vast number of people who have helped me along the way.

A million thanks to my agent, Steven Chudney, who is equal parts hilarious and dedicated. You always know the right thing to say, and it usually makes me laugh. For that, and for loving this story, I will always be grateful.

To my editor, Erica Finkel, who fell in love with these characters and their story, and worked so hard to make them the best they could be. Any time you're ready to vacation at the lake, Minnesota and its sky-blue waters are here for you. To the team at Amulet, including jacket illustrator Sean Scheidt and book designer Alyssa Nassner, thank you for helping make this book so beautiful.

Countless thanks to my critique partners and readers for your thoughtful notes, timeline charts, and endless support. Dawn Klehr, you've been with me from the beginning and I couldn't have done this without you. Kari Marie White, thank you for write-ins, coffee, and your exquisite attention to detail. Erin L. Schneider, thank you for loving Ben and Lulu so much and for your keen observations. Thanks to the MNYA Writers, who saw very early sections of the book and are still cheering me on.

Elodie Nowodazkij and Adrianne Russell, thank you for reading and for your boundless encouragement. Rebekah

Faubion, thanks aren't enough for your friendship and belief in me and this book. Stephanie Elliot, thank you for always being just a phone call away and for your amazing knowledge of soda brands (and pineapple).

So many thanks to the young adult and middle-grade authors of the 2017 debut group. You are all amazing, wonderful people, and I'm so glad to be on this journey with you.

Thank you to Linda Diaz, Sara Naegle, and Maris Ehlers for being my biggest fans, long before this novel even came to be. Your support and enthusiasm mean the world to me. And thank you, Maris, for my gorgeous headshots. You're in a league of your own.

I owe Chad Talbot a huge debt of gratitude for selling me an old laptop—cheap—when I was in desperate need. I wrote and revised many versions of this book on what's affectionately known as "The Chad." Thanks to DJ Hartley for giving me time and space when I needed it. And to Karen Carlson—I wish you were here to read this. I miss your laughter and your wit.

I am so very grateful for the friendship and support of the UMD Gang over many years: Jacqueline Bonneville, LeeAnn Evans, Heather Green, Katie O'Dell, Jana Oman, Jody Rittmiller, and Teresa Robinson. My life has been infinitely better with all of you in it.

Huge thanks to Jeff Evans for your incomparable fishing knowledge and your willingness to answer all my questions, no matter how basic.

To my siblings, nieces and nephews, and in-laws—thank you for believing in me and cheering me on. Thank you to my parents, Ted and Terry Biren, for being the first people to support my dream of becoming an author, and for sending me to writing workshops and summer camps and graduate school. Mom, thank you for being my biggest cheerleader. And Dad, I wish you were here to see my novel on the bookstore shelf. I miss you every day.

Thanks to my writing instructors: first, Joseph Maiolo at UMD, who said I had "the gift." You were a bright light in my world, I learned so much from you, and you are missed. Thanks also to MSU's Richard Robbins and Roger Sheffer, and especially Terry Davis, who encouraged me to write YA.

My children have never known a time when their mom wasn't writing or on deadline for one thing or another. Thank you, Jude and Halen, for thinking it's cool that your mom is a writer, and for your constant love, hugs, and encouragement. Hold on tight to your dreams.

And all of my deepest gratitude and love to my favorite: my best friend and husband, Troy, who has never once faltered in his belief in me. You are an inspiration to me every single day.